"You didn't
Cord remi...

"Brooke Hollister," she said, then slammed the door as hard as she could and shot the bolt.

"Nice name—Brooke," he called after her. "Like a cool drink of water." From the tone of his voice she thought he might be smiling now.

That she could hear him so well through the closed door was disconcerting. This meant the walls must be thin and he could eavesdrop on her if he had a mind to. Not that she had anything worth hiding—except her pregnancy. And that wasn't something she intended to talk about for some time. To anyone. At least not at Rancho Encantado, Where Dreams Come True.

How nice it would be if dreams really did come true here. But that was all hype. A handsome cowboy appearing on one's doorstep could be a dream come true for some people; however, it certainly wasn't for her. Even if he did have impossibly wide shoulders, slim hips and sexy hazel eyes…

# BABY ENCHANTMENT
## Pamela Browning

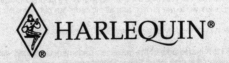

TORONTO • NEW YORK • LONDON
AMSTERDAM • PARIS • SYDNEY • HAMBURG
STOCKHOLM • ATHENS • TOKYO • MILAN • MADRID
PRAGUE • WARSAW • BUDAPEST • AUCKLAND

This book is dedicated to my dear friend Carolyn Swallow,
whose innate spirituality is always an inspiration.

ISBN 0-373-16994-9

BABY ENCHANTMENT

Copyright © 2003 by Pamela Browning.

## ABOUT THE AUTHOR

Pamela Browning has written many books for Harlequin American Romance, but this is the first one she's ever researched by being caught in a dust devil in Death Valley. Fortunately, the dust devil didn't accompany her to her sailboat, where she wrote much of this book. Pam lives with her husand in a variety of places—don't ask. Just read her next book.

She invites you to visit her Web site at www.pamelabrowning.com.

**Books by Pamela Browning**

### HARLEQUIN AMERICAN ROMANCE
818—THAT'S *OUR* BABY!
854—BABY CHRISTMAS
874—COWBOY WITH A SECRET
907—PREGNANT AND INCOGNITO
922—RANCHER'S DOUBLE DILEMMA
982—COWBOY ENCHANTMENT

Don't miss any of our special offers. Write to us at the following address for information on our newest releases.

Harlequin Reader Service
U.S.: 3010 Walden Ave., P.O. Box 1325, Buffalo, NY 14269
Canadian: P.O. Box 609, Fort Erie, Ont. L2A 5X3

*Near the California-Nevada-Arizona*
*border in the year 1910*

The dry desert air has preserved the scroll well, though the ink has faded to brown.

"What is it?" asks the young rancher, who cannot read a word of Spanish.

"Ah," answers the elderly priest with a twinkle in his eye. "It contains an old legend telling the reason that we call this place Rancho Encantado—the enchanted ranch."

The rancher shuffles his feet in the dust. "Well, Padre Luís, we thought it was a pretty name," he replies. His bride waves fondly from the window of the old adobe hacienda, one of several buildings on their newly purchased spread in the desert area known as Seven Springs.

"A pretty name? Yes, I suppose it is. But this place received that name because good things happen here. Unusual things, unexplained things."

"Like what?"

"Just…things. But they are things that touch the soul."

"Oh. Well, it's good of you to tell me. But this legend of yours sounds like so much guff." The rancher is eager to escape the priest, who arrived unexpectedly to hand over the land deed and the Spanish scroll. He is glad for the school and hospital that Padre Luís founded here, but he and Betsy have no need of the school yet, and he hopes they will never need the hospital.

The priest seems eager to explain. "The legend came about because of what happened at Cedrella Pass back in 1849 during the gold rush. A lot of people died there in the old days when the West was being settled. A Shoshone woman took it upon herself to reverse the curse."

"You mean there could be something special in the water?"

The priest raises his eyebrows. "*Quizás.* Perhaps." He smiles mysteriously and winks. "But more likely, it's something we always carry with us, something wonderful, something within the human heart."

While the rancher is mulling over this pronouncement, the priest hoists his bulk up onto his mule. "Remember, this is a special place," he says.

The rancher stands watching as the rotund priest rides down the dusty track that serves as a road. Then, with a shrug, he rolls up the parchment and heads for one of the outbuildings, unused at present except for storage.

He'll toss the parchment scroll into one of the old trunks there. Then he'll forget about it. He has a ranch to run, after all, enchanted or not.

# Chapter One

Brooke couldn't believe it, but at the same time, she didn't think the pregnancy test would lie. Just like the ads on TV, the strip showed two pink stripes, meaning that she was pregnant. Preggers. Knocked up. The dismay she felt hit her hard in the pit of the stomach, which reminded her that now she knew why she felt like tossing her cookies every morning. She stared at the bright Southern California cityscape outside her bedroom window, her bleak feelings at odds with this sunny March day in L.A.

The phone rang, yanking her back to reality, and she almost didn't answer. It could be Leo, she supposed, and she knew he wouldn't welcome the news that he was going to be a father. Nevertheless, she scooped up the handset and clicked it on.

"Hello?"

It wasn't Leo but Felice Aronson, features editor of *Fling*, the number-one magazine for young women on the West Coast. She sounded out of breath. "Brooke, I'm glad I caught you. Something has come up, and I hope you don't mind rescheduling our lunch for eleven o'clock instead of noon.''

Brooke often wrote articles for *Fling,* and she was prepared to pitch several ideas to Felice today. ''Something has come up here, too, Felice. How about next week?''

''Sorry, Brooke, I can't. I'm leaving for Mexico City on business tomorrow afternoon.''

Brooke's heart sank. How could she present her ideas—or herself—in a positive light with pregnancy weighing on her mind, not to mention her heart? She was still smarting over last week's breakup with Leo, she had no idea how she was going to raise a child on her own and she was on deadline for an article for *Redbook.* But Felice was her favorite editor as well as a friend, and they had business to discuss.

Brooke closed her eyes against the pink-stained pregnancy strip and tried to focus on lunch. ''Okay, Felice, I'll meet you at eleven.'' Maybe her roiling stomach would settle down by then.

''Right. *Ciao,* Brooke.''

Brooke hung up and sank onto the bed. Leo's picture grinned at her from her dresser on the other side of the room. It had been taken in happier times, before he'd decided that he didn't want to be saddled with a wife, kids, a dog and a mortgage. Before he'd broken up with her. Before she'd wanted to crawl into a hole and die.

Now there was a baby to think about, and she couldn't summon any benevolent feelings toward it at all. She felt only bewilderment, sadness and pain at this turn of events in her life. Where would she and the baby live? Her apartment was hardly big enough for one. Who would take care of the baby? As a free-lance writer, she worked at home. Getting any work done with a baby around was hard to imagine.

The scene outside, all palm trees and tile rooftops, blurred. She was thirty-three and had never been married. She had hoped to be a wife, Leo's wife. That was never going to happen. And now she knew without a doubt that she was going to be a mother.

A baby wouldn't fit into life as she knew it. Motherhood was definitely the last thing in the world she wanted.

FELICE ARRIVED at their usual table at the trendy Beverly Hills restaurant looking svelte, tanned and enthusiastic. She had returned three weeks earlier from a Hawaiian vacation, where she had picked up information about a fantastic health spa-dude ranch located in a valley surrounded by desert in southeastern California.

"The Rancho Encantado motto is 'Where Dreams Come True,'" Felice said as she nibbled on the leaf and matchbox-size bit of tuna that were her lunch. "Apparently, there's something to it, because people come away from there with not only a makeover but a life. Honest, that's what I've heard."

Distracted as Brooke was over the results of that morning's pregnancy test, she barely registered the information. She needed to jockey for a conversational opening in which she could insert one of her own article ideas, such as the one about female bodybuilders or another about men afraid to commit. She could write a whole book about that one, probably.

"Mmm," she said, staring down at her plate of quesadillas, complete with spicy salsa and a heap of guacamole. Although she craved anything spicy these days, the very thought of eating something slimy and green made her stomach lurch.

"The thing is, I don't believe the hype, either. The owner of Rancho Encantado is a former model, Justine Somebody, who used to run the Razzmatazz Agency in New York. There's reputed to be an old Indian curse...it's part of the lost legend."

"What lost legend?"

"No one can remember what the legend is, and the curse is supposedly responsible for the bad things that happened there. But then the curse was reversed—"

"You're kidding, right?"

"No, that's what they say. Oh, and the place is supposed to be the location of a vortex," Felice told her.

"I didn't realize *Fling* was into New Age."

"We're not. The point is that this Justine is probably really good at public relations or knows someone who is, and she's made up all these stories to draw people to the place. Maybe you can poke a hole in the puffery, Brooke, and find out what Rancho Encantado is really about."

"I was thinking that my next *Fling* article should be about female bodybuilders," Brooke said faintly.

Felice dismissed this idea with an authoritative wave of her hand. "They're passé, at least as far as *Fling* is concerned. But makeovers are still in. Everyone wants a makeover."

"Not me," Brooke said. She was about to be made over, all right. Pregnancy was going to transform her into a pudgy, waddling version of herself, and there wasn't a whole lot she could do about it.

"That's too bad, Brooke, because I figured you could wangle a free makeover out of the assignment. Not that you need it. I wish I had your naturally blond hair and cute figure because I'm sick of hairdressers who don't do what I ask and diets that don't work."

"Thanks, but I could use some dieting pointers."

"I'll let you know about my current diet after I weigh myself tomorrow. It's all too, too depressing." Felice shoved her plate aside with a look of distaste.

"Suppose I find out that Rancho Encantado lives up to its promises and can't write the piece the way you want it? What then?"

"So do what you want. All I'm saying is that I think the article would be better if you had firsthand knowledge of what they do there."

Brooke considered this. "Where exactly is Rancho Encantado, anyway?"

"Near the California-Arizona-Nevada border, a few hours' drive from L.A. and two hours north of Las Vegas."

"Isn't that near Cedrella Pass—the gap in the mountain range where people traveling to the goldfields died on their way to California during the gold rush in 1849?"

Felice shrugged. "I can barely keep up with current events much less history."

Brooke tried to remember the oft-repeated family lore about her ancestors' big move from the East to

California. "My great-great-great-grandmother Anna-bel Privette was traveling with a wagon train and died on the infamous Tyson Trail because the wagon master misjudged the weather and they got snowed in at Cedrella Pass with very little food. I've always thought the story would make a great book."

Felice brightened. "There you go! Use this assignment to check the story out. Even if it's not book material, you might get a couple of good articles out of it. Say, aren't you going to eat your lunch? It's on me today."

"I'm not hungry. Blame the early lunch hour and a late breakfast, okay?" Not the whole story, but it would do for now.

"So will you take the assignment? Please say yes!" Felice was at her most persuasive.

"Well—" Brooke began, but Felice interrupted.

"I'll toss in a couple hundred dollars more than we paid for your last piece, and you get a vacation out of the deal. And," Felice said craftily, "there's the small matter of an interview with Malcolm Jeffords."

"What interview?"

"The one he's considering giving *Fling.* We're in the final stages of negotiation for a profile."

Malcolm Jeffords was a rock star who had grown up singing gospel with his six cousins, some of whom had gone on to become almost as big a star as he was. Despite his large fan base, his career had hit the skids a couple of years ago after police broke up a raucous party at his house. They had taken several partygoers into custody, including a couple of monkeys. Jeffords had retreated behind the high walls of his estate in the

Hollywood Hills; he had never talked about the incident publicly.

Brooke was wary of Malcolm Jeffords. He had the reputation of being both controlling and hard to interview. "You're saying what, Felice?"

"That I want you to write the profile. Only you could do it justice."

"Um, what do you mean?"

"Well, you *have* written an article about monkeys for the Sunday section of the *L.A. News.*"

"That was about sociological research using primates, not about monkeys sliding down water slides with a certain difficult rock star."

"I was trying to be funny."

It was sort of funny, but today Brooke was seriously lacking a sense of humor. "All right, so you're giving me the Jeffords interview, provided I get the scoop on Rancho Encantado first, right?"

"You could say that. Both these articles are important to me, Brooke. They could be important to you, too. If Jeffords goes through with the interview, we'll up our print run. It'll be big, really big."

A large print run. Major exposure. TV interviews to follow, plus her phone would ring off the hook with calls from other editors, wanting her to write about topical subjects.

Brooke didn't have to think about it any longer. "All right, I'll do it," she said abruptly. The Rancho Encantado deal had fallen right into her lap and would be easy money, which was important since she'd be supporting two from now on. And the Jeffords interview would be a major coup.

Felice grinned and called for the check. "Okay, Brooke, we've got a deal. I'll call you when I've set up the Jefford's interview. By the way, you're lucky to be going to Rancho Encantado right now. The desert isn't as hot at this time of year as it is in summer. Warm days, cool nights. You'll love it. I'll give you the Rancho Encantado phone number and you can make the arrangements yourself." She dug a slip of paper out of her purse and handed it to Brooke.

Brooke tucked the paper into her briefcase, pushed the quesadillas across the table so that she wouldn't have to smell them and excused herself to go to the rest room, where she blotted her face with a wet paper towel. Maybe the nausea would have abated by the time she left for Rancho Encantado.

And maybe not.

THREE WEEKS LATER, on the next to the last day of March, Brooke was on her way to Rancho Encantado in her sporty red Miata, a map unfolded on the seat beside her.

On the map, Cedrella Pass didn't look like any big deal. With her fingernail, Brooke traced the dotted line that indicated an unpaved track and then ran her finger over to the nearby green spot that sat in the middle of the desert in the area known as Seven Springs. Rancho Encantado was not only a health spa and dude ranch but also a working cattle ranch, according to the woman she'd spoken with on the phone. Since Brooke was going to write an article about the ranch, she would have a free room, a makeover and access to any part of Rancho Encantado that struck her fancy. As

Felice had pointed out, you could hardly beat that deal with a stick.

When Brooke emerged from the mountains bordering the western boundary of the desert, it was as if she had entered a whole different world. The undulating golden hills seemed to radiate a warm light, and their gentle folds wrapped her in a welcoming hug. Although the desert was arid and austere, the road led her into a green and fertile valley bisected by a narrow stream; the sky was a brilliant blue and unsullied by clouds. Ahead, like a mirage, lay a cluster of low buildings—Rancho Encantado: the enchanted ranch.

The entrance to the ranch was framed by two rock pillars topped by a sign bearing the ranch's name and the motto Where Dreams Come True. A sign pointed her toward a registration building and a rec hall.

Brooke parked her car and went inside the building marked Registration. There she joined a long line at the check-in desk. Apparently, she'd arrived on the busiest day of the week, and there was considerable hubbub due to the many new guests. The confusion didn't stop her, however, from idly listening to the conversations around her.

"I heard that Rancho Encantado is located on the site of an earth energy center," said a woman in front of her. "A vortex, it's called."

Brooke recalled that Felice had also mentioned a vortex. She quickly dug her reporter's notebook out of her briefcase and began to take notes.

"So what's a vortex?" demanded the woman beside her.

"I'm not sure."

Another woman pitched in. "It's a geophysical anomaly. People have tried to explain the biochemical changes that occur in people when they visit vortexes, but so far no one is sure what happens. Scientists would like to be able to define the physics of the energy centers, and they've tried to in such places all over the planet by measuring magnetic fields and electrical impulses that may or may not be present."

"Have they had any luck?"

"Nothing conclusive, although they've noticed that such energy centers are all heavily charged with negative ions, even in the most arid climate conditions like the ones here in the desert."

The first woman shrugged. "Don't get so technical, Dolores."

"Yeah, and none of that explains the Rancho Encantado ghost," said another.

"Ghost? There's a ghost?"

"They say that the place is haunted by a priest named Luís who built a school and hospital here," someone chimed in.

"Oh, great. Ghosts, yet. Geez, all I really care about is that I lose a few pounds, get a new hairstyle and enjoy a break from my four kids."

"Amen," said one of the others, and they all laughed.

The line began to move faster, and Brooke wrote down *"check on ghost"* before tucking her pad away in her briefcase. Soon she had reached the desk, where she filled out a card and received a packet of materials. Suitably equipped with information, she exited the building, stopping just outside the door to consult the site map for directions to her room. As she shuffled papers and maps and brochures, a thick cream-colored envelope fell out of the packet. She ducked to pick it up at the same time that a shadow fell across the porch.

She glanced up and saw a man outfitted in full cowboy regalia scowling down at her. He was a big man, a rugged man, with high bony ridges to his cheekbones and a jagged scar blazing across his chin. He wore his Stetson pushed far back on his head.

"Excuse me," she said, embarrassed. "I'm a bit slippery-fingered today."

The scowl deepened. The man shifted his booted foot and, with a ripple of muscles underneath his tight-fitting shirt, bent to pick up the flyer he had trampled. "Here," he said gruffly. "Could be important."

The paper was something to do with yoga lessons, but that barely registered as she took in the long leanness of his thighs, the tautness of the faded jeans stretched across low-slung hips. "Thanks," she said. "Can you point me toward the guest quarters? I'm staying in—" and she consulted her registration packet "—Desert Rose."

"That way." He jerked his thumb at a cluster of buildings beyond the date-palm grove, clearly a man of few words.

"Thanks again."

He grunted, cocked an eyebrow and continued into the Registration building as she stared after him. He walked purposefully, and she sensed rather than saw a stiffness to his carriage. His physique was arresting, but his curt demeanor and the scowl on his face detracted from his rock-jawed good looks. Not that he was the type to care.

"Are you Brooke Hollister?"

Distracted from her thoughts, she whirled around to face a strikingly attractive woman with one long silver-blond braid hanging down her back.

"Yes," she said. "And you?"

"Justine Abbott," said the woman as she held out a slim hand.

After Felice's assessment Brooke was unprepared to like the owner of Rancho Encantado, but Justine's smile impressed her as friendly and genuine.

Justine gestured toward the envelope in her hand. "That's an invitation to a wedding tonight at my house, the Big House. Perhaps you'll want to come. My brother is getting married, and everyone's invited."

"Why, I—" Brooke's first inclination was to decline, soured as she was on happily-ever-afters these days.

"The wedding will give you a chance to get acquainted with people who can help you with your article. I think you'll enjoy it."

"Then I'll be there," Brooke replied, all hope for a leisurely evening fading.

"Good," said Justine, favoring her with a cheerful grin before striking off in the direction of the rec hall.

Brooke watched her as she went, and then she headed toward Desert Rose. The building consisted of four suites grouped around a courtyard, each with its own private entrance. The rock garden in the center of the courtyard was planted with cacti, carefully landscaped and groomed. For a moment she caught a glimmer of light emanating from the center of the cactus patch, but after a closer look, she decided that she'd been mistaken. Her vision must be affected by the bright desert sun, she thought, or perhaps the thin air.

When she inserted her key in the door to her suite, it swung open to reveal a surprised older woman sitting across the room, thumbing through a magazine. As Brooke stared in dismay, the woman leaped from the couch as if she had seen, well, a ghost.

"Who are you?" the woman demanded, drawing her blue Rancho Encantado robe around her.

"I'm sorry if I startled you, but I'm Brooke Hollister. They told me that this was to be my room."

"Your room? When I've been here since yesterday?" Keeping a wary eye on Brooke, the woman strode across the carpet and swept the phone out of its cradle.

Brooke flourished her key as proof. "I just came from the check-in desk."

The woman seemed to soften. "Well, I'll have to ask you to wait outside while I call the desk."

By this time, Brooke was feeling decidedly queasy, perhaps because she'd grabbed a hot dog for lunch along the way. "All right," she said. She supposed you couldn't be too careful who you let in your room.

The woman treated her to a penetrating look. "Are you okay?" she asked suddenly. The expression in her eyes was kind and concerned.

Brooke wasn't sure, but she said, "I think so. I'm surprised, that's all."

"As I am. We'll get this straight, don't worry." The woman smiled reassuringly.

Brooke, fumbling in her pocket for a Tums, wheeled her suitcase outside again and cooled her heels beside the Joshua tree that provided minimal shade for a very pregnant gray cat who glared at her disdainfully. "What's the matter?" Brooke asked the cat. "Are you annoyed with me, too?"

The cat stared at her for a moment, then proceeded to wash her face with her paw. The cat's bulging sides reminded Brooke of her own pregnancy. As if she could forget it, especially now that she had told Leo.

"You what?" he'd said when she'd confronted him in the foyer of his apartment building. He'd looked as shocked as she'd expected, was as furious as she'd known he'd be.

"I'm pregnant," she'd repeated flatly, and with that he'd hustled her into the elevator and up to his apartment without a further word. She should have felt some emotion at seeing that familiar space again, at the sight of the furniture she had helped Leo choose for the life she'd expected them to spend together. But instead, all she felt was a sense of failure and a deep sorrow that things hadn't worked out the way she'd hoped.

"Sit," he'd barked, and she'd sat, whereupon he'd stalked to the bar and poured himself a stiff drink. He hadn't offered her one, either by intention or oversight, but she couldn't have swallowed anything anyway. Leo's hands were shaking as he seated himself across from her.

"You're not going to have the baby, of course." He spit out the uncaring words.

Her head shot up. "Of course I am. It's my baby—*our* baby," she corrected herself.

"How do I know that?" He narrowed his eyes and didn't conceal his quick assessment of her figure, which had not yet begun to show her pregnancy.

"Don't be ridiculous," she retorted. "You know I've been entirely faithful to you the past two years."

"We've been apart since January."

"This is March. I'm almost three months along."

"You took precautions."

She shrugged helplessly. "They didn't work."

He tossed back the rest of his drink, and as he got up to refill his glass, Brooke, feeling curiously aloof, spotted a bit of red lace peeking out from underneath one of the couch cushions. She reached over and tugged at it, then held the item up so she could see what it was. With a jolt of recognition, she realized that she was staring at a thong in a size smaller than she wore. In her shock, she tried to stuff it back under the cushion, but Leo saw. He turned pale, which only underscored the incongruity of the situation.

She stood. "I don't think we have anything else to discuss, Leo," she said. "I'll be going now."

Leo blinked, but not before she detected the negative emotions flitting across his features. Anger, arrogance, denial, even fear.

Brooke wasn't surprised. After their bitter breakup, she hadn't expected more than this, and she'd long suspected that he fooled around with other women. "I don't want any help from you, now or ever," she said, drawing the tatters of her dignity around her like a protective cloak.

"Brooke—"

"No, Leo. Let's end this with as few recriminations as possible. Don't worry, I won't be sending you a birth announcement." With that she had walked away, head held high, and let herself out of Leo's apartment for the last time.

Her confrontation with Leo had happened only yesterday, yet it was a lifetime ago. Perhaps it was, in a way. Her new life was just beginning, a life in which she would be responsible for a baby. The obligations this would entail were staggering. Struggling to meet those obligations without the support of the man she'd loved seemed even worse.

"Ms. Hollister?"

She whirled to see the woman whose suite she had entered beckoning from the door.

"You're to go back to the check-in desk and they'll find other accommodations for you. I'm Joanna Traywick, by the way, from Albuquerque. I hope there will be another suite to your liking."

Brooke forced an agreeable nod, but she hated inefficiency, especially when it affected her.

Joanna smiled at her. "I'm really very sorry if I was rude, but you startled me. All this talk about ghosts, you know."

If the situation hadn't been so awkward, Brooke might have inquired into the matter, but as it was, she only assured Joanna that she didn't hold her responsible for this inconvenience, inadvertently backed into a cactus as she tried to swivel her luggage around on the path and soon was on her way to the Registration building.

All she wanted was a space to call her own for the duration of her stay. She was ready to put her feet up and relax while she continued to reconcile herself to the new realities of her life.

THE PERSON IN CHARGE of registration was a small scurrying woman named Bridget, who appeared stressed to the max by the large number of arrivals.

"I'm so sorry, Ms. Hollister," she said as she worriedly leafed through a card file. "This wedding has put a strain on our facility. I could put you in the building we call Salt Grass—but no, I'm afraid that's impossible. The bride's relatives are staying there. Perhaps—oh, dear. I'm afraid someone has made a terrible mistake. Everyone is assigned to a room, and we're full up."

Brooke felt a stab of dismay. She wouldn't have driven all the way out to the desert on this day if she hadn't been promised a room.

"Perhaps there's a place in town." She knew that the closest town was Sonoco, miles away and across the Nevada border.

Bridget looked scandalized. "Oh, that's impossible."

"There must be a hotel."

"I'm afraid not."

"A motel?"

"No."

"No place to stay at all?"

One of the women who had been talking with the

informative Dolores earlier in the check-in line was standing next to Brooke at the counter. "Only Miss Kitti-Kat's, and I don't think you'd want to stay there." She gave a little laugh.

"Oh, why not? Maybe they have a room."

"Honey," said the woman, dropping her voice, "it's not a regular hotel. It's a—a house of ill repute, if you know what I mean. They're legal in Nevada."

"A brothel," Brooke said.

The woman nodded knowingly, and Bridget looked distinctly uncomfortable.

"What's going on here?" Justine strode out of an adjacent office and frowned at Bridget, who began to explain. She omitted mention of Miss Kitti-Kat's, which was probably just as well.

After hearing her out, Justine shooed Bridget away. "Brooke—may I call you Brooke? Don't worry, we'll make room for you at Rancho Encantado. How about my brother's apartment? It's small and adjacent to the stable, but it's quite comfortable."

"I can hardly put him out of his own place," Brooke said, though at this point she wasn't sure she cared.

"Hank has moved to the old hacienda that he will share with his bride once they come back from their honeymoon. His former apartment has been refurbished with an eye to housing one of my staff eventually, so all is in order. Bridget, please show Brooke where she'll be staying."

Justine must have sensed her disappointment, because she touched her arm and said, "I know it's not what you expected, but you'll have access to the spa, the oasis hot pool and our makeover services. In a way, you may like the suite better. You'll have your own kitchen, too.'' Justine smiled reassuringly.

''What about a place to plug in my computer and get online?''

''Yes, the apartment is equipped for that.''

There seemed to be nothing to do but grin and bear it, so Brooke gritted her teeth and followed Bridget, who kept up a nonstop stream of nervous and innocuous chatter all the way to the stable.

Brooke was pleased to discover that the apartment was newly painted and furnished in a southwestern cottage style. The chairs in the living room looked as if they had recently been slipcovered in natural-colored linen, and a soft afghan lay folded on the couch. A Navajo rug, old and faded to warm shades of coral, blue and gold, covered most of the plank floor, and the television set was hidden away in a large antique pie safe. She was glad that the small kitchen afforded a view of the mountains in the distance. Brooke couldn't complain, she thought as she hung her skimpy wardrobe in the closet. This place was a freebie, after all, and the switching around had ensured that her pregnancy hadn't crossed her mind for oh, at least an hour.

That was progress, she thought grimly.

She looked for the place to plug in her computer near the desk in the bedroom but found only one phone plug, and that belonged to the phone on the bedside table. Well, maybe she would be better off not to check her e-mail yet. She didn't want to read any angry messages from Leo.

She stripped down to her bra and panties; and, because her breasts were tender with pregnancy and uncomfortable, unhooked her bra and slung it over a doorknob. Then she crawled in between the sheets to catch a nap. The pregnancy made her sleepy nearly all the time, and this little apartment was far enough away from the other guests to afford her plenty of nap time.

She fell asleep immediately, and she didn't awake until she heard footsteps on the wooden floor followed by a curse.

"Damn!" said a man's voice. "Who are you?"

She struggled up in bed, holding the thin sheet over her breasts. The man was the cowboy she had met on the porch of the Registration building, and his light hazel eyes were spitting fire.

"I believe we've met," she said levelly and coolly. "But since I don't care who *you* are, please get out."

He held up his hands in a gesture of peace. "I'm Cord McCall, the ranch manager, and I've got no desire to rile any naked ladies. I'll get what I came for and be gone."

"I'm not naked," she said, regretting her words immediately.

"Couldn't tell it," Cord said, a wry twist to his mouth as his gaze drifted to her bare shoulders and below. She was positive he could see her nipples puckering beneath the thin sheet.

He backed out of the room and she heard him walk into the kitchen, where the refrigerator door opened and closed. She scrambled out of bed and yanked a robe out of her open suitcase, then dropped it over her head, inserted her arms in the armholes and zipped up the front. By the time she had rushed into the kitchen, Cord McCall was popping the next-to-the-last can out of the plastic six-pack of beer on the table and twisting the tab upward.

"Want one?" he asked.

"No. All I want is to know how you got in. My assumption was that these were my private quarters."

"Door," he said, glancing sideways. Sure enough, there was a door. It appeared to lead into an adjoining apartment much like this one.

He tipped his head back and let a long swallow of beer slide down his throat. Looking directly at his Adam's apple, she couldn't muster the anger that she thought she should feel.

"You can slide the lock after me when I go back to my place if you want," he said.

"I certainly will," she said tightly. His eyes were a complex mix of gold and brown, and his gaze didn't leave her face for even a moment. They wore her out, those eyes. They seemed to know too much.

He didn't smile, didn't even try to look friendly. "Sorry for the intrusion. I've been using the fridge in here since mine went on the blink. Didn't think anyone would be in here."

He gave her a casual salute as he picked up the last beer and headed through the door.

"You didn't tell me your name," he reminded her as she moved to shut the door after him.

"Brooke Hollister," she said, then slammed the door as hard as she could and shot the bolt.

"Nice name—Brooke," he called after her. "Like

a cool drink of water.'' From the tone of his voice, she thought he might be smiling now.

That she could hear him so well through the closed door was disconcerting. This meant that the walls must be thin and he could eavesdrop on her if he had a mind to. Not that she had anything worth hiding, except her pregnancy. But that wasn't something she intended to talk about for some time. To anyone. At least not at Rancho Encantado, Where Dreams Come True.

How nice it would be if dreams really did come true here. But, she reminded herself, that was all hype. A handsome cowboy appearing in one's bedroom could be a dream come true for some people; however, it certainly wasn't for her. Even if he did have impossibly wide shoulders, slim hips and sexy hazel eyes that seemed to feast upon her body.

## Chapter Two

Cord McCall, sitting in the back row at the Big House, where the wedding between Justine's brother, Hank Milling, and his bride, Erica Strong, was in progress, thought Brooke Hollister was sexy as hell. He couldn't figure out for the life of him what someone with her big-city polish was doing here at Rancho Encantado. The last thing she needed was a makeover, in his opinion.

He couldn't help feeling slightly melancholy over all the cheery sweetness and light surrounding this marriage. True, the makeover had done wonders for Erica, but Hank had confided that the reason they were marrying was that they were well matched intellectually, something that Cord couldn't fathom. You either had a lech for a woman or you didn't. Forget the touchy-feely stuff; forget the soul-mate thing. The only place for all that was in cheap novels.

Up front, Hank and Erica were kissing. A big long kiss, and it was embarrassing to watch. Cord didn't like public displays of affection, even at weddings. He glanced away, and his gaze fell on Brooke Hollister, who was fidgeting two rows in front of him. Maybe weddings made her feel uncomfortable the way they did him.

As the bride and groom faced their guests to be introduced as husband and wife for the first time in their lives, Cord was struck by the joy of this new beginning. That was what weddings were about—beginnings. Perhaps Hank had the right idea in marrying; Cord had never had the luxury of becoming intimate enough with any woman to take that major step. The truth was that he had suffered too many endings in his life, too many wrenching goodbyes. The realization plunged him into a gripping sadness, one that he was pretty sure would linger until long after bride and groom had left under a shower of rose petals.

And then the happy couple were walking arm in arm down the aisle, on their way to the tent outside, where the reception would be held.

Hands stuffed deep in his pockets, Cord wandered over there, uninterested in talking to any of the ranch hands or registered guests, who were also on their way to the tent. After he had mumbled his way through the reception line, he spotted Brooke standing alone off to one side. He'd have thought she would have found someone to talk with by now. Yet she didn't seem interested in any of the other guests. She looked so forlorn that he found himself drawn in her direction and wondering if she felt as out of place with this crowd as he did.

"Excuse me, but would you happen to know where the ladies' room is?" Brooke asked as he drew closer. Her complexion was distinctly green, and before he could answer, she blurted, "Never mind," as she bolted toward a flap in the tent. He stared after her. He'd dealt with too many hangovers not to recognize the unmistakable signs of someone who was about to upchuck.

Moodily, he pulled out one of the white chairs set up for the occasion and straddled it, knowing that this was not good manners but not caring, either. He was here and decked out in a suit and tie for only two reasons: Justine was his boss, and if she took it into her mind to throw a wedding for her younger brother, why, he was duty-bound to attend. And he genuinely liked Hank, though the two of them had little in common. He'd figured Hank would have been offended if he hadn't come to the wedding.

While he gulped a glass of champagne more rapidly than he should have, Cord scanned the crowd. The bride's sister was gorgeous, but she was a six-foot-tall supermodel and intimidated him big-time. Their other sister was also beautiful, obviously married to the man who had accompanied her, and they had a child in tow. As for Justine, she was busy trying to pull off a wedding dinner with a chef who was temperamental, and she kept running in and out of the tent with a harried expression on her face. Cord figured he'd cut out before they served the pheasant under glass, or whatever.

Without warning, the tent flap lifted and Brooke Hollister ducked in. She sank onto the chair beside him, shaky but composed.

"Feeling better?"

She shot him a sharp look out of the corners of her eyes.

"No need to deny it. I recognize the signs of a hangover."

Her eyebrows raised. "Voice of experience?"

"I've nursed a few in my time." He paused, figuring that if he didn't continue the conversation, she'd eventually get up and move away. But he felt guilty about the way he'd treated her so far, so he cleared his throat. "What I always do is drink lots of water. Seems to help."

She nodded. "I suppose it counteracts dehydration."

"Exactly."

She didn't say anything more, and then a waiter walked by bearing a tray of champagne flutes.

"Champagne?" Cord offered, copping another one. Brooke held out her hand to take a glass before quickly snatching it back.

He nodded in approval. "Hair of the dog—it's the worst thing you can do," he told her. "Wait here. I'll get you some water."

"Oh, but—"

"No problem." He got up and wended his way through the tables to the bar. When he returned, Brooke was checking her lipstick in a mirror.

"Thanks," she said as he handed her the water.

He noticed that her eyes were large and bright, almost too big for her face. They were blue shading to lavender, an unusual shade, and deeply fringed by long dark eyelashes. The green in her complexion had faded to a creamy pallor, and her cheeks now showed a tinge of pink.

Their hands brushed as she accepted the glass of

water from him, and he thought he detected a shimmer of interest in those unusual blue eyes before it was quickly veiled. Several other guests found their way to the table, and in order to avoid having to make conversation with people who were out of his element, he figured that, since the band struck up a tune, he might as well ask Brooke to dance.

"Not that I'm all that great a dancer, mind," he warned her while she preceded him onto the minuscule dance floor.

"Neither am I," she confessed as he took her in his arms, liking the way she kept her distance. He was accustomed to making brief command appearances at the weekly Rancho Encantado square dances and having middle-aged guests get a mite overfamiliar.

She was wearing a simple, belted dress, nothing fancy, in a becoming shade of aqua. He'd hoped she wouldn't try to talk to him, but once they were dancing, she seemed to talk nonstop.

"What does a ranch manager do?" was one of her questions.

"Too damn much."

"That's not exactly helpful," she admonished.

He angled away from her. "Helpful for what?"

"For the article I'm writing."

"What article?"

"About Rancho Encantado."

He rolled his eyes. "I should have guessed. Justine wouldn't put a regular guest in a stable apartment."

"It's very comfortable, except for intruders."

Somehow, he wasn't surprised that she'd bring this

up. "If I'd known you were nursing a hangover, I wouldn't have made so much noise."

Of course, she realized. He thought she'd been sleeping it off this afternoon.

He raised a conspiratorial eyebrow. "It's okay. I won't tell anyone."

"There isn't anyone to tell, and I'm a big girl."

The glance he spared her was appreciative and took in her breasts, barely visible above the scooped neckline of her dress. "I noticed."

"I didn't mean—"

"Never mind." He drew her closer.

She pushed him away slightly. "How long have you been the ranch manager?"

"Too damn long."

"All right, so you don't want to tell me anything. Who else will talk to me?"

"Most anyone, I reckon."

"I've hardly met anyone else."

"Is that my fault?"

She rolled her eyes. "Maybe." He sensed that she enjoyed sparring with him.

"So what should I do? Stop dancing with you?"

"If you like."

"I don't." He pulled her closer again. She smelled of exotic perfume, musky and sophisticated.

She pushed him away for the second time. "You could let me know to be on the lookout for certain people. For instance, who is this Ananda, the yoga instructor? Do you see her here?"

"Nope. She's probably contorted herself into a pretzel out in the middle of the desert as she contemplates her belly button.''

''Do you suppose that's possible? Contorting into a pretzel shape while contemplating your navel?''

Unexpectedly, he threw back his head and laughed. Several heads swiveled in their direction as he subsided into a long chuckle. ''I think I'd rather contemplate yours,'' he said.

She flushed and bit her lip. ''Don't make suggestive suggestions,'' she said. He suspected that she was about to laugh. The corners of her mouth twitched beguilingly, and the idea popped into his head that he wanted to kiss her.

''I suggest that we duck out of this party and make our own fun,'' he said.

''I'm not sure what your definition of fun would be,'' she said primly.

''I'll be happy to show you.''

''You know, I would like to get some fresh air. It's stuffy in here.''

''I'm for that.'' He stopped dancing and took her hand in his. It nestled there, and he fought an unfamiliar protective urge swelling up from somewhere. He held the tent flap for her and followed her into the cool night air without a backward glance.

''Just a minute,'' he said, dropping her hand. He tugged at his tie to loosen it and unbuttoned the top button of his shirt.

''If you can do that, I can do this,'' she said, unfastening her belt a notch. He considered this a good sign. Women didn't usually loosen their clothing unless they were agreeable to removing parts of it.

She wrapped her arms around herself, shivering. "The nights are chillier in the desert than I expected at this time of year. I should have brought a wrap."

He removed his coat and slid it around her shoulders. "Better?"

"You didn't have to," she said.

"I wanted to." He took pleasure in the familiarity that giving her his coat implied, and the hope flitted through his mind that when he got it back, it might smell of her perfume.

They walked along the path, and he said, "Have you explored the ranch much?"

"Not at all," she replied. She didn't look up at him, and that was bad. Eye contact was a big part of a proper seduction, and he was determined that this was going to be a seduction, the more improper the better.

"Why are you writing about Rancho Encantado, anyway?"

"It's an assignment," she said.

"Newspaper? Magazine?"

"It's for *Fling*. That's a woman's magazine published in L.A."

"I know what it is. And what it isn't."

She appeared intrigued by this answer. "What isn't it?"

"You'll be offended." She was staring up at him, at his scar. He hated the scar on his chin, but it was part of him. A branding of sorts.

"No, no. I won't. I promise. I'm only a freelancer. I don't own the magazine or take any responsibility for its content."

"My impression of *Fling* is that it's junk-food reading. Lots of calories and no nutrition."

She laughed. "That's very insightful."

He had never known a woman before who used words like *insightful*. "Thanks."

"Is that all you're going to say?"

He knotted his forehead and glanced in her direction. They were walking along the fence line, the stars bright above, the mountains to the east hiding the moon.

"It's enough. I don't want to insult you."

"No insult. It happens that I agree with you. I can't imagine your reading *Fling* to begin with."

He'd been introduced to the magazine in the doctor's office after his accident. During his recuperation time, he'd devoured everything in print. Books, newspapers, magazines and, when his eyes tired, books on tape. He hadn't been able to do much else at the time. Work wasn't possible, and after breaking his back, he'd thought he could never ride a horse again. But he could, and he did.

"Is it such a surprise that I read?"

She considered this. "Of course not. I've always associated cowboys with more of an outdoor life, that's all."

"What's your favorite book?" he retorted.

"It's always the last one I've read," she said. "What's yours?"

"I don't have a favorite, but if I did, it would be about the history of the Old West."

"That would make you something of an authority on the subject, right?" she said as they approached the

Big House. Once past it, they turned down the path that led to the stable.

"Nope," he said. Far behind them, they heard the band starting up again after a break. Somewhere, glass broke. He was glad they had left the reception.

They walked on in silence, their footsteps crunching on rock.

"So what else do you do in your spare time?" she asked after a while.

"Just…things." For some reason he would have liked to tell her about Jornada Ranch, but he sensed that this wasn't the time or the place.

"Things," she repeated. He detected a note of annoyance.

Eager to dispel it, he said in a low tone, "It's not what you think."

She angled her head toward him. "What could that be?"

Her scrutiny made him uncomfortable, but her skin looked soft and touchable. His fingers itched to touch it, and he wondered what she would do if he lifted his hand and traced a finger along her jaw. He clenched his hands, promising himself that there'd be time for that later.

"You'll hear rumors," he said. "People talk."

"About you?"

He shrugged. "If not me, someone else. Better me, I guess. I can take it."

"You're a tough guy, huh?"

"I'd say so."

They had reached the stable, and he said on a sudden inspiration, "Would you like to meet the horses?"

"Sure," she said. He wasn't certain that she was really interested, but he led her on the rounds of the stalls: Tango, Stilts, Sebastian, Melba, Whip and his own horse, Tabasco.

Brooke seemed taken with Stilts, a spirited chestnut gelding. "This is the one I want to ride," she said.

"You ride?"

"I used to go to horse camp every year between the ages of eight and sixteen. Then my parents bought me a horse. They still have him. If I want to ride, do I need to reserve the horse or anything?" she asked.

"There's a sign-up sheet," he said. "I'll show you."

He opened the tack-room door. "There's the sheet," he said, pointing to the clipboard hanging from a nail.

She followed him into the tack room and positioned herself in a corner beside a wall hung with bridles and bits, looking small and waiflike under the dim light from the ceiling fixture. Someone so delicate seemed out of place in that room, with its smells of leather and horse and hay, seemed at odds with all the equipment pertaining to horses.

"Of course, you'll need to be checked out by me or one of the ranch hands to make sure you and the horse are suited."

"Stilts reminds me of my own horse, Dexter. He and I will get along fine," she said. She somehow brushed against the bridles and set them to swinging. "I—I'd better be getting back to the apartment," she said.

He didn't think she meant it. "Don't do that," he

said softly, captivated by the shadows of her eyelashes on her cheeks. Slowly and seductively, his gaze slid down to where her breasts swelled against the fabric of her dress.

"Cord," she began, but he moved in closer and eased his hand up one of her arms.

"Like I said, we don't need to leave yet."

She stared at him, and it dawned on him that she hadn't expected this. But perhaps she was only playing coy.

"We have a long night ahead of us," he said, keeping his voice low and casual. "We could shorten it considerably if we had something to do."

"Stop," she said, her voice full of bewilderment. "I didn't want—this."

Surprised, he let his hand fall away.

"I'm sorry. I'm preoccupied, and I didn't realize that you—" Shé broke off in midsentence, letting the words hang there. She seemed to pull herself together before suddenly pushing past him and out the door.

"Brooke, wait," he called, pivoting to follow her, but she was running past the stalls toward her apartment.

"Brooke?"

She stopped on the steps and rummaged in her purse. "I must have dropped my key," she said. "I didn't even notice."

He kept his distance, even though the door to his apartment was adjacent to hers. "Brooke, I hope you aren't angry."

"I'm going to go look for my key along the path," she said distractedly.

"You can go into your place through mine. They do adjoin."

She glared at him. "If that's your way of trying to get more friendly than I had in mind, forget it." With a toss of her head, she marched out of the stable and between the row of eucalyptus trees toward the path that would lead her back the way they'd come.

Cord stood staring after her, wishing she'd given him back his jacket before she'd taken off. This was his only suit, and he took good care of it. He would have taken good care of her, too, if she hadn't gone as skittish as a pregnant cow.

He waited for a few seconds, wondering whether to follow her, and quickly decided that it wouldn't be a good idea. Anyway, he was hungry and ready for a snack. He let himself into his apartment. Suddenly, he remembered that he didn't have access to a working refrigerator anymore. The damn thing had quit on him last week, and the repairman had lots of excuses about why he couldn't show up, not the least of which was that Rancho Encantado was a fifty-mile drive from his place of business. No matter; Cord would be going on vacation next week. Maybe the fridge would be fixed by the time he got back, and maybe not.

He settled into his favorite armchair to watch television while he waited to hear the opening and closing of the door to the neighboring apartment when Brooke returned. But she didn't come back. After almost an hour, Cord began to be alarmed. If she'd really dropped the key on the path, her search shouldn't have taken this long.

In Cord's estimation, Brooke Hollister was city

smart, but she was alone here, out of her element. It occurred to him that perhaps he was responsible for Brooke after all. With a sigh, he went into his bedroom and changed into a pair of jeans and a shirt. Sometimes, a heifer took it into her head to ramble off. Often, she got herself into trouble. When that happened, he had to go round her up, and that was what he'd better do with Brooke Hollister. Round her up. Bring her in. Make sure she stayed safe even if he was the last person she wanted to find her.

*MEN!* Brooke thought as she stormed back along the path toward the Big House. She'd believed that Cord was different, considering how helpful he'd been. She hadn't thought he wanted to hit on her, and she'd let down her guard. With the reality of her pregnancy weighing heavily on her mind, she stupidly discounted the signals that he was coming on to her.

As for that lost key, even though she kept a tiny flashlight on the ring with her car keys, it still took her longer than she'd expected to find it. Finally, there it was, a metallic gleam amid a clump of grass beside the path.

She tucked the key into the outside pocket of her purse and kept walking along the path, thinking that she shouldn't have left the wedding reception. She stopped near the Big House, trying to decide whether to go back to the reception. It was early, only nine o'clock. She could stay for an hour, mingle and keep her antennae out for information that she could use. It might be a good idea to eat something, too.

The very thought made her stomach churn. She

fumbled in her purse for the saltines that she'd started carrying with her at all times, since she'd read in a newspaper column that they were good for nausea.

But she hadn't brought them. She had transferred the necessities—lipstick, wallet, comb—into a much smaller clutch bag when she'd dressed for the wedding. The package of saltines wouldn't fit.

And she was still wearing Cord's suit jacket. If she was going to return to the reception, she'd have to go back to the apartment and find something else to wear over her dress. And she didn't have anything that matched.

Unfortunately, she heard the clink of metal on rock. Oh, great—she'd dropped the key again and the flashlight, as well. As she bent and scrabbled among the weeds at the edge of the path, Cord's jacket trailed in the dust, which made her realize that she was going to have to offer to pay for dry cleaning. She didn't want to talk to him ever again, and as her stomach started to heave, she realized that she was going to have to talk to him, like it or not. Mostly not.

She felt awful. The nausea came in waves, worse than she'd ever experienced it, but her fingers closed around the barrel of the flashlight and she quickly found the key. By the time she stood up, she was overcome with the unfairness of life. She had loved Leo, and she had lost. Her emotions were balanced on a fine edge, and she felt herself slipping into a state that, if she were writing about this experience, she would describe as overwrought. Her nose was running, and her eyes were tearing up, and she thought she might be sick after all.

Some people were walking along the road, and she recognized none of them. She knew, however, that she didn't want them to come across her while she was sniffling and feeling sorry for herself, so she looked wildly around for someplace to go. There was what appeared to be a walled garden in the rear of the Big House, and much to her relief, the gate was open. She slipped inside, relieved to see a bench where she could rest for a moment.

The moment became several minutes, and the tears became sobbing, and all she could think as she huddled there beneath Cord's jacket was *Oh, God, dear God, what am I going to do about this baby? And what about* me?

BROOKE WAS SO WRAPPED UP in her troubles that she almost didn't hear the click of the gate latch. She leaped to her feet, ready to run.

"Easy," said Cord, letting the gate swing closed behind him. The mellow glow of the house lights behind the windows fell upon his face and struck golden glints in his dark hair. He stood with his hands hooked through his belt loops and looked taken aback at her tear-stained face.

She sank onto the bench. "What—what do you want? I told you not to follow me."

"Why? So you could cry in private?"

She blotted at her eyes with a tissue. "No. Crying was not what I thought I'd be doing."

His mouth quirked. "It does seem like an overreaction to losing your key."

"I wasn't—oh. You're joking."

"I'm trying to find out what's the matter."

"Nothing you would understand."

He crossed the flagstones in two steps and sat down beside her. "I guess you're right."

She stuffed the tissue into her purse. It wouldn't close.

"Did you find the key?"

"Yes."

He thought about that. If she wanted to talk, he'd let her, though he didn't relish the idea of listening to all her problems. He wouldn't be able to summon anything but boredom if she wanted to speak of love gone wrong, or arguments with her girlfriends, or any of the other mostly inconsequential things that women cried about.

"I know you must think I'm overemotional," she said in a low tone.

He shrugged. "Maybe."

"The truth is that I feel weepy all the time. It's not the way I usually am. I can usually take things in stride. But now...." Her voice trailed off, and he considered that maybe he should suggest walking back to their apartments. He forced himself not to look at her, though she didn't look half-bad even with her eyes all red and her makeup washed away by tears.

"I should never have come to Rancho Encantado," she said miserably. "I'm not in any state to be working."

"I'm not sure what you mean," he said cautiously.

"I mean—oh, I don't know what I mean. I have to work. I have no choice now."

It was the "now" that caught his attention. Did she

mean that she hadn't always had to work? That she'd had a choice prior to coming here? And why was that so, if it was?

She went on talking, her tone reflective. "Sometimes, you have your life all wrapped up in a little box, pretty paper, nice bow. Then the bow unravels, and the paper crumples, and inside the box is a bunch of stuff that you never expected."

Cord could identify. His life had been about rodeos. Then a tractor-trailer rig had careered out of the night and changed all that. He was lucky he wasn't a paraplegic. A broken back was a major injury.

"The thing is, can you ever tie the bow back up again, uncrumple the paper? I keep wondering." She sighed.

"Depends," he said.

"Even if what's in the box is something totally different from what you expected?"

"Different doesn't mean worse," he said. His life now wasn't worse than his old life. It was different. He hoped it would be more meaningful.

"I never thought I would be in this situation," she said. "Never."

"What situation?" He didn't like women who never got to the point. Usually, that is. But he liked Brooke. He couldn't help himself. Something about her appealed to him, and he didn't know if it was her manner, which was mostly defensive, or the thinly veiled vulnerability that he sensed beneath the veneer of sophistication.

He had avoided looking at her face, not wanting to intrude on what privacy she had. But now he focused his gaze on her eyes and saw with unease that they were filling with tears again. This was getting way too sticky for him, and he wished he hadn't looked.

"Oh, there's no point in—"

"Brooke," he said more gruffly than he intended, "you remind me of a skittish mare, wanting to get friendly but ready to bolt at any minute."

"I can see why you'd say that. I'm not myself lately, that's for sure." She managed a rueful quirk of her lips that could have passed for a smile if he hadn't known better.

"Well, why not?"

"I just found out I'm pregnant," she said, her voice very quiet.

*Oh, hell,* he told himself, wishing he had stayed in his apartment and watched TV, instead of coming after her. The last thing he needed in his life right now was a pregnant woman, and that was the truth.

# Chapter Three

Sitting beside him in the garden adjacent to the Big House, Brooke noticed that Cord's boots were thick with dust. One of her tears fell on the right one, which was crossed over his knee. The tear ran in a runnel and dripped from the sole to the ground. Brooke wiped her eyes again, wishing she could stop crying. This pregnancy had turned her into a real waterworks.

"You're not happy about being pregnant," he said. It was a statement, not a question.

"I should be," she said miserably. "Once it would have been the best news in the world."

"I see," he said.

"Then—but I don't want to get into that."

"So when is the baby due?"

"In about six months."

"That's a long time."

"It doesn't seem like it," she said doubtfully. She forced herself to rally. "You know, I've got to start thinking about this in positive terms. I've just begun to regard it as a baby, not a nuisance. A baby should be welcome. Its arrival should be an occasion for happiness. I'm shortchanging this child by not feeling joy over it.''

"True,'' Cord said, looking pensive and gazing off into the distance.

"So,'' she said, "I'd better buck up.''

"Sensibly said.''

"If I can.''

"You seem like a strong woman.''

She glanced over at him. "I was. I can be again.''

"Good attitude.'' He stretched and said, "You want me to walk you back to your apartment, or would you rather walk alone?''

She bit her lip. "I'd like the company. I'm sorry if I was rude earlier.''

"Maybe I'm the one who was rude. I shouldn't have hassled you. I thought you wanted what I wanted.''

"No.''

"All right. Let's call a truce.''

"Fine.''

"Want to shake on it?''

He was halfway surprised when she hesitated, then stuck out her hand. It was cool and soft, and for some odd reason, a picture sprang into his mind of her hand smoothing his forehead after a long day at work. This was ridiculous in the extreme. What could have put such an image into his head? It wasn't the kind of thing he usually thought about.

She stood up. "I haven't mentioned to anyone that I'm going to have a baby. Would you mind keeping it a secret?''

"Won't be too hard. I'm not in the habit of gossip.''

"I didn't think so." She shot a tentative smile up at him, and his jacket fell off her shoulder. He reached over and adjusted it for her.

They fell into step with each other, keeping a fair distance between them. The sky was filled with stars. They gleamed against the backdrop of the night, the Milky Way clearly visible in an endlessly drifting path. The sky was so vast, the stars so bright, and Brooke was reminded how insignificant her problems were in the grand scheme of things.

Perhaps there was a reason for her pregnancy, a reason that this baby should be born. What if her child could perform some valuable service to humankind? Save the world? Or, forget saving the world—there were lots of things that needed doing on this planet. Curing the common cold. Or figuring out how to make nations get along with one another. Or teaching people how to read, for heaven's sake.

"You're smiling," he said. "Want to tell me what's so funny?"

She had forgotten momentarily that he was walking beside her. She told him her thoughts, and to her surprise, he threw his head back and laughed. It was a delight, that laugh, deep and wholehearted. Somehow, she'd gathered that he didn't laugh much.

"I guess I'm trying to make myself feel better about this mess," she admitted.

"That's okay. It's a mental exercise that will give you the strength to cope."

He spoke so seriously that she shot a questioning glance at him. "You sound like the voice of experience."

"Maybe."

They were close to the stable now, and they walked on in silence. A coyote howled somewhere in the direction of the old abandoned borax mine that she'd seen as she drove onto the Rancho Encantado property, and she shivered. The cry was such a lonely sound. It reminded her that she was alone, and she didn't want to be.

As they approached the door to her apartment, Cord said uneasily, "See you tomorrow, I guess."

"I'll be hard at work."

"Get your mind off what's troubling you."

"Yes."

"Well, then, good night." He turned toward his own door.

"Cord?"

"Yes?"

"Would you like a cold drink? I bought some things at the little store next to the Registration building before I went to the wedding."

"I see," he said.

"I—I didn't know if your refrigerator had been repaired yet."

He put one booted foot on the bottom step and stared at her. She hoped he hadn't taken her offer the wrong way.

"As it happens, the fridge is still on the fritz. I'd appreciate very kindly something cold to drink."

"Come in," she said as she swung the door open and led the way.

She stood blinking at him uncertainly in the cold

light of the overhead fluorescent. "What would you like? I bought a bottle of wine. Some lemonade, too."

"Should you be drinking wine? Pregnant women usually give up alcohol."

She flushed. "I wasn't thinking. Like I said, I'm not used to the idea yet." She attempted a laugh. "I'd better stick with the lemonade."

"Wine for me." He sounded as if he didn't care for wine much.

"I'm sorry I don't have beer."

"That's okay." He stood looking irresolute.

"Won't you sit down. I have some crackers and cheese. I wasn't hungry before, but now I regret not eating at the reception."

He sat and pushed a chair away from the table while she got out two glasses and poured wine for him, lemonade for her. Her back was to him as she spread cheese on crackers, so she wasn't looking at him when he cleared his throat and said, "The father of the baby isn't around, I take it."

"Oh, he's around. Not around me, that's all." Her tone was brisk, but she still felt bruised and depressed over her encounter with Leo.

"It doesn't sound as if you have any feelings for him," Cord said.

She brought the plate of crackers and cheese over to the table and sat down across from him. She took her time replying.

"The only feelings I have for Leo now are disgust and pity, which is distressing to me. I wanted to marry him. Now I see it's impossible, and I think a child needs a father in his life.'' She blew out a long breath. ''This baby will never know its father, and that's sad.''

Cord took a gulp of wine and set his glass down on the table. His fingers traced the base of the glass, and he seemed to be thinking. ''You're right,'' he said at last. ''A child should know his father. Life isn't so easy for kids without parents.''

He usually spoke abruptly, even gruffly, so his thoughtful tone grabbed her attention. He seemed very intense, focused, even a bit pensive.

''Is that a firsthand observation?'' She didn't know what made her ask; something in his expression, perhaps, or his voice.

''It's not important.''

Even as he made the statement, she knew that it *was* important, and in a uniquely personal way. That he was trying to evade discussion clued her in to his inner turmoil about the issue. She had often been told that she was good at empathizing, and now she intuited that there was more to this than Cord wanted to admit.

She decided that self-revelation might be the key to finding out more about what Cord wasn't saying.

''I was fortunate,'' she said. ''I came from a two-parent family. I learned how lucky that was when my cousin Tim moved in to live with us after his father skipped out on him and his mother. His mom couldn't support him, so he was with us for five years. He tagged around after my dad like a lost little puppy, wouldn't let him out of his sight. Tim had been in trouble. He'd started experimenting with drugs and was picked up for shoplifting a couple of times. He straightened out when he began to see my dad as a role model.''

Cord looked interested in spite of himself. ''What happened to Tim?''

''He's mayor of the little town where we grew up. He has a wife and two kids, is a model citizen.''

''That's a great story, Brooke.''

She smiled. ''It is, isn't it?''

''Not every boy in trouble has the good luck to find someone like your dad.''

''No.'' She felt a pang of sorrow for the new little life that she harbored in her belly. ''I only hope my child won't suffer because his father doesn't want anything to do with him.''

''If a child has one caring parent, that's enough. You'll be a good mother, Brooke.''

She drained her lemonade. ''I wish I could be sure that I'll be a good mom. I'll do my best. I know that.''

Cord's eyes flickered for a moment with an emotion that she would have translated as tenderness if she'd thought he was the tender type. ''You'll do fine.'' He finished his wine, and she offered him a refill.

''I'd better be on my way,'' he said. He stood.

''Before you go, can you tell me where I'm supposed to plug in my computer? There's no plug near the desk.''

He looked chagrined. ''That's my fault, I reckon.''

''Your fault?''

''I was supposed to move the desk from the bedroom to the alcove in the hallway after the phone guy finished his work. Want me to do it now?''

She shrugged. ''Sure, if you don't mind.''

She led him into the bedroom. He flicked his eyes momentarily toward the bed, then jerked a thumb at the desk. "Bring the lamp, okay?"

She picked up the lamp, and he hefted the small desk as though it had no weight at all. She followed him to the alcove, and he set the desk down.

"Electrical outlet on the right, phone outlet on the left, and once you're plugged in, your computer will be ready for work and for e-mail."

"Thanks, Cord."

"Don't mention it." He headed for the kitchen, but she was right behind him.

His hand was on the outside doorknob.

She spoke quickly. "No need to go out that way. You can nip right over to your apartment through the adjoining door."

"Guess I could, if you don't mind."

She went and unbolted the door, then held it open. All of a sudden, she remembered his jacket, which she'd slung over the back of a kitchen chair when they'd come in. "Wait a minute. Here, you'd better take your coat with you. I may have gotten it a bit dusty. Maybe I'd better have it dry-cleaned."

He held the jacket up and inspected it. "Nothing that a good brushing can't fix."

"You're sure?"

"Positive. Anyway, with any luck at all, I won't have to wear it again anytime soon. I'm not much for fancy dressing."

She liked the way he looked in his jeans, western shirt and cowboy boots, but she thought he might be uncomfortable if she said so. "I appreciate your taking care of me tonight."

"It wasn't much."

For a moment she thought he wanted to say something more, but she must have been mistaken.

"Good night," she said.

He didn't say good-night, only nodded abruptly.

After he had gone back into his own quarters, she closed the door behind him and bolted it. The thought occurred to her that she should have asked him if he wanted to keep a few things in her refrigerator until his was working again. For a moment she considered knocking on the door and asking him, but she was afraid that he was thinking that he was well rid of her after hearing all about her pregnancy and putting up with her emotional outbursts.

FOR SOME REASON, Cord couldn't get Brooke Hollister out of his mind. He lay awake staring at the ceiling for hours, unable to sleep. Not until he woke up the next morning did he realize what the problem was, and when it finally occurred to him, he rolled out of bed with a curse and went into the kitchen to start the coffeemaker.

His mother might have been just like her. Like Brooke Hollister. And the thought gave him chills.

Not that he'd ever known his mother. She'd borne him in secret and turned him over to his father shortly thereafter. She'd been unmarried, like Brooke. She'd had a profession, like Brooke. Only, his mother's profession was something he didn't like to think about much.

The coffee slid down his throat, thick and hot. It made him feel better, or at least more alert. He was preparing to ride out to check on the cattle in the far pasture, when the phone rang. He yanked the receiver from its cradle, annoyed with the interruption. "Yeah?"

"Bucky?"

"You got him." Not too many people called him Bucky anymore; that name was part of his past.

"Bucky, I thought I'd better check with you. We've got a kid who needs a home real quick. You any closer to opening that place of yours?"

He recognized the person now. It was Ted Petty, the judge who had given him a chance all those years ago.

"Ted, good to hear your voice. I've been working as hard as I can, but Jornada Ranch is still weeks away from licensing."

"That's too bad. This kid could be a winner, but he's in a bad home situation and I'm worried about him."

Cord sat down, his forehead furrowing in concern. "Is he in physical danger?"

A pause. "I don't believe so, but there are other problems in his home. Brandon has an alcoholic father, a mother who keeps running off with various men, and his sister was recently sent to juvenile detention. So far he's okay, but he'd benefit from the kind of place you're going to have—I'm sure of it."

Cord passed a hand over his eyes and blew out a long breath. "I hate to hear of these things, Ted. Believe me, I'd do anything I could for Brandon. But the ranch isn't ready yet.''

"Listen, Bucky, you call me if you need any help with the licensing. I can rush things through the proper authorities.''

"I appreciate that. Look, how about if I let you know when I have an opening date?''

"Fine. That would be good.''

"Ted, I'm sorry I can't help you yet.''

"It's okay, Bucky.''

But was it really okay? Cord knew it wasn't. It wasn't okay as long as that boy had to live with a father who drank too much and a mother who was worse than none.

After they hung up, Cord thought about the kid this judge wanted to help. He pictured him as a scrawny boy with straggly hair and eyes that reflected a whole lot of painful memories. How did he know what this boy would look like? Because he himself had been like that once. He had been that kid.

He tossed the dregs of his coffee into the sink. Long ago, he had learned that the best thing to make him forget present wrongs and old wounds was work. Fortunately, that was what his life was about these days.

He clapped his hat on his head and strode out into the stable, angry at the world right now and not afraid to show it.

THAT MORNING, Brooke was up early. She threw on some clothes and let herself out into the stable. It was very early, and no one was around. The dry air was cool and crisp; she felt invigorated by it. She went to say hello to Stilts, wishing that she had an apple or a carrot or a sugar cube to give him.

At the sound of Cord's door closing, she turned quickly. He had stepped out of his apartment and was walking toward her through the slanting rays of the early-morning sun.

"Good morning, Cord," she said. "Do you keep any sugar cubes around? I'd like to give one to Stilts. It might make us friends."

"In the tack room," he said. He walked past her and yanked a saddle down from its perch. Without saying another word, he strode into Tabasco's stall and led him out to be saddled.

His curtness surprised her. She thought they had parted friends last night. "Mr. Congeniality," she muttered, but Cord heard her.

"What's that?" he asked sharply.

"Nothing," she said. She let herself into the tack room, found the sugar and put a couple of extra cubes in her jacket pocket before she went back to Stilts's stall.

After she'd fed Stilts the sugar, she walked to where Cord was saddling his horse. His eyebrows were set in a surly line and the corners of his mouth turned downward.

"Cord, do you want to check me out on Stilts, or should I ask someone else to do it?" she called to him as he swung into the saddle. She thought she saw him wince when he mounted, as though as he was in pain.

"Sal will arrive here in a few minutes. Talk to him." His abrupt tone irked her, and just for the heck of it, she stepped out into the sunlight and squinted up at him, shading her eyes with one hand. In the eucalyptus trees a bird sang cheerfully, the mellow notes a stunning counterpoint to Cord's expression.

"Have I done something to offend you?" she asked.

He stared down at her for a long moment. "Nope," he said.

"I mean, you've been awfully cross with me. I know I was a lot of trouble last night. I'm sorry. I'll try not to bother you again."

His expression hardened. "Look, everything isn't about you." Tabasco danced toward the corral gate, and Cord reined him in.

Hurt, Brooke stepped back from the dust cloud the horse's hooves had stirred up. "I don't think *everything* is about me," she said. She wished she hadn't pursued this conversation.

"I guess I didn't mean that the way it sounded," he said. "I've got a lot of stuff on my mind right now, that's all."

"Well, so do I," she retorted.

"Right. You do. Look, this isn't a good time to talk about all this. I've got to go, Brooke. There's work to do."

She bit down hard on her lower lip in order not to say something she'd be sorry for later. She watched him as he rode out of the corral, lost in a blur of dust before he reached the curving road leading to the working part of the ranch.

That was what she got for thinking they were friends, she thought to herself as she went back to Stilts's stall. She could use a good friend right now, but clearly Cord McCall didn't intend to be one.

"So maybe you and I will be buddies, huh, fella?" she said as she stroked the horse's soft nose. He nudged her shoulder, undoubtedly hoping for another sugar lump. At least, Brooke thought as she dug one out of her shirt pocket, Stilts wasn't as grumpy as the redoubtable Cord McCall.

CORD TRIED HIS BEST not to worry about Brandon. It wasn't easy, though. The kid was on his mind as Dusty, his second-in-command, briefed him on ranch business for the day, and he couldn't stop thinking about the boy as he rode over to the shed where they kept the pregnant cows. Brandon was still on his mind when he dismounted and looked inside.

There was one cow who seemed edgy, and Cord identified her as one of those that could go a little crazy giving birth. She lowered her head and snorted at him, backing away as he approached.

Cord eyed the recalcitrant heifer with a baleful eye, almost as baleful as the look she was giving him. Cows, he reflected as he hauled the calf-puller out of the storage room, were the stupidest animals on the face of the earth. This one was even stupider than that.

March was the beginning of calving season, and the pregnant cows had to be checked every two hours around the clock. Justine had a considerable investment in this herd, and she didn't want to lose any mothers or babies. Of course, he assigned the hands to keep tabs on the pregnant cows, but on certain occasions, whoever was delegated the task had other things to do. Cord, being the working ranch's manager, was where the buck stopped.

The heifer made a distrustful *hoomphing* sound, and a couple of the cows that had calved last night stopped chewing their cud and turned their heads to take in the situation. Then they turned away again, apparently satisfied that whatever was going on, it was no threat to them or their babies.

Cord wished he'd called in one of the other guys for help. This heifer was now swaying frantically, in labor and furious with someone, anyone. It was her first calf, and she obviously didn't know what to expect or whom to blame.

"Don't glare at me," Cord told her. "I didn't get you into this."

The heifer bawled at him, nervously eyeing the coiled-up lasso in his right hand.

"Easy, Daisy," he said. Cord had no idea whether this cow's name was Daisy or not. More than likely she didn't have a name. He called all female cattle Daisy; it made things simpler.

He studied her for a moment, deciding that he might as well get this over with. He sent the rope zinging through the air, and Daisy shied away as the loop fell neatly over her head. She rolled her eyes wildly and continued to bawl. A scuffle ensued, and he almost couldn't hold her. The exercise played havoc with his back, and he felt something wrench. That wasn't good, but he shut the pain out of his mind. That was all he could do sometimes: shut the pain out.

Finally, he managed to snub the line around a post, and when he wasn't sure that one would hold her, he lapped it around a second post. Meanwhile, Daisy fought.

"I want to help you," he told her between gasps for air. "We're gonna get this over with, and you're gonna be fine."

Daisy gave no sign that she believed this. Instead, she pulled so hard against the rope that her eyes bulged and her tongue stuck out like a sausage. Finally, without warning, the cow collapsed onto the hay.

He played out the rope, and her eyes and tongue returned to normal. No sooner had he regained his breath than she leaped up and he had to tighten the rope again. This wasn't cruel, in his mind. Letting Daisy give birth all alone with no one to help her in case of trouble, at the mercy of coyotes, which preyed on newborn calves, would be crueler. Finally, Daisy fell down upon the hay again, he loosened the rope and she gave him a look that could be interpreted as one of gratefulness. He smoothed her face for a minute, and she was as docile as could be.

He sometimes grew impatient with the length of the cows' labor, but on the other hand, gestation for a cow was nine months, just as for a human. He figured he could wait around as long as it took for the calves to be born.

Daisy set about giving birth as energetically as he'd ever seen, and when the calf finally appeared, he was able to pull it in no time. It was a beautiful little animal, black like its mother. He wiped mucus from its nose and dipped the navel in iodine, and when one of the guys looked in to see how things were going, he gave him the job of making sure the calf began to nurse within the next couple of hours.

Because of his back injury, tending to Daisy had made him ache all over. He kind of liked caring for the pregnant cows and appreciated the miracle of birth, but he'd never told anyone. It might make him seem like a sissy.

When he was finished at the calving shed, he rode over to the barn and went inside to find out if the group he'd sent up to Dragon Canyon had returned from rounding up stray cows. As he strode into the barn, a random thought hit him: Brooke was going to give birth to that baby she was carrying, and no wonder she was apprehensive about the pregnancy. He had never before related what cows went through to the ordeal that women experienced, but wasn't it the same thing? Pain? Misery?

For a woman to give birth to a baby that she wanted might be one thing, but if she didn't want the baby, it must be a lot harder.

"Hey, boss, you know anything about that load of hay that was supposed to be delivered?"

He was forced to turn his attention to management matters, but he couldn't get the thought of Brooke's pregnancy out of his mind for the rest of the afternoon. No wonder she was upset. She had a lot to deal with and, from the looks of it, no one to help her through it.

Still, birth was a miracle. Maybe she needed someone to remind her of that.

He'd been a little hard on her this morning. He hadn't meant to be. It was as he told her, he had a lot on his mind and didn't feel like commiserating or relating or whatever.

Anyway, he was going on vacation next week. Keeping his distance from Brooke Hollister was probably a good idea. Ending whatever was between them before it had begun was an even better one.

LATER THAT DAY, Brooke treated herself to a self-guided tour of Rancho Encantado, courtesy of the guidebook provided at check-in. The grove of date palms, planted in the 1920s as a commercial venture that hadn't panned out, sheltered a number of pools that gave the Seven Springs area its name.

Beyond the palm grove was the building that housed the recreation and dining halls, and up the hill in the distance, she could make out the old borax mine, closed now. She could barely spot the tamarisk trees that screened the hacienda, the original homesteaders' house, from the road.

She scrawled a reminder to ask Justine if she was welcome to poke around in some of the old outbuildings and hurried to lunch, where she joined a group at a table in the dining hall. From across the room, Joanna Traywick, the woman she'd disturbed when she'd walked into her suite in Desert Rose, gave her a friendly nod. No hard feelings, apparently. Maybe Brooke would chat with her later and tell her that she'd ended up in the apartment and liked it.

Most people in the dining hall seemed to be eating rabbit food. Brooke was no exception; she ordered a salad, thinking about the inevitable weight gain that went along with pregnancy. Leo didn't approve of overweight people. He— But why did she care what Leo thought? He was out of her life.

The women in the group were Dolores, the talkative woman from the check-in line at registration, and her friend Tracey, who had informed Brooke about the true nature of the Sonoco establishment known as Miss Kitti-Kat's Teahouse. The other two at the table were Linda and Kate, sisters from Texas, who said they vacationed at Rancho Encantado every year.

"And do you find it to be true that you not only get a makeover here, you get a life?" Brooke asked.

Kate, who was eating something resembling a slice of lentil loaf, spoke up. "Last year, Linda got a makeover *and* a life for a while. One of the cowboys visited her in Dallas."

"He was there to visit his brother, and we only went out three times," Linda explained quickly.

"Still, it was more than you expected when you met him at the square dance," Kate reminded her.

"Yes, well, he married someone else six months later." Linda sighed and prodded her meager salad as though this might produce something more substantial—shrimp, or perhaps a bit of chicken.

"Is that common? Romance between the ranch hands and the guests?" The wedding of Hank and Erica was still on Brooke's mind. They'd looked so happy, and she'd overheard in the ladies' room that Erica had been a guest at the ranch; Hank worked here.

"The hands are encouraged to give the guests a good time, but I don't think they're supposed to follow them home. Too bad, because I've seen one I'd like to lure back to Texas," said Linda.

"Who's that?" asked Dolores.

"The mysterious Cord McCall," Linda said with an air of intrigue.

"Oh, don't bother," Kate told her. "He shows up at the dances because he has to, and we've never noticed him taking an interest in anyone."

Dolores and Tracey exchanged glances. "We've heard all sorts of gossip about him," Dolores said.

"Oh, great," said Linda with a groan. "Maybe I'd better set my sights on someone else."

"You might want to take a look at the guy called Stumpy," said Tracey. "He's almost as good-looking, and he doesn't have a scar."

"I like Cord McCall's scar," said Linda defensively. "It lends character to his face."

Brooke, who had followed the exchange with much interest, dug into her salad without enthusiasm. She hadn't expected an instant rundown on Cord McCall. She'd put him out of her mind after their brusque encounter that morning.

Yet now, even though she didn't want to, she was thinking about him again, and the idea of his paying visits to a brothel made her distinctly uncomfortable.

*It's not like that,* said a voice in her ear, and she quickly turned to Kate to see if she had spoken the words. But Kate had her mouth full of lettuce and celery and was crunching audibly. For a moment, Brooke saw the chubby figure of a priest shaking his forefinger at her in admonition, but when she blinked it went away. What she had thought was the priest was only one of the waitstaff hurrying across the room with a pitcher of water.

"Are you quite all right?" someone asked her, and

Brooke glanced up to see Joanna Traywick standing beside her. She stared as if the woman were an apparition, as well.

"Why—um, I think so," she said unsteadily.

"I was passing by, and you looked so pale. I'm a medical doctor. If you need any help, let me know."

"You're very kind," Brooke said.

Joanna touched her shoulder. "Call anytime."

*Does pregnancy make you see things that aren't there? Does it make you hear things that no one said?* She would have liked to ask those questions, but Joanna had already headed for the door, and the others were now discussing their makeovers.

Brooke turned her attention back to the conversation, but she discovered that she wasn't nearly as interested in the colors of nail enamel the manicurist offered as she was in other aspects of Rancho Encantado. Such as visions of priests that came and went. And a cowboy named Cord McCall.

AFTER LUNCH, Brooke stopped by the Registration building for a hurried conference with Justine, who gave her unlimited access to all records, outbuildings and personnel at the ranch.

"No problem," Justine said. "Go anywhere. Look at anything." She went to a file cabinet and pulled out a folder full of newspaper clippings. "I don't know what's in here," she said. "It's a jumble of things someone collected. I found the folder when I took over the ranch. You might come across something of interest in it. If you'll stop by the Big House tomorrow

morning, I'll let you borrow some books that might
help, too.''

The file bulged with information, and at last Brooke
began to feel positive about this assignment. The
folder's contents would certainly help provide background information about Rancho Encantado, and
there might even be something about the Tyson Trail
and the Cedrella Pass incident.

As she cut through the stable on her way back to
her apartment, deep in thought about her work, she
almost ran into Cord McCall, who was emerging from
the tack room. He seemed to be in a different mood
from the one he'd been in that morning. In fact, he
actually had a cheerful expression on his face.

''Whoa!'' he said, reaching out and steadying her.
His hands lingered a bit longer than necessary on her
shoulders, or was it her imagination?

''I'm sorry,'' she apologized. ''I should have been
looking where I was going.''

''No apology necessary. About this morning,
Brooke—''

''No apology necessary there, either,'' she said
tersely.

''Okay, be that way.'' She detected an unexpected
mote of humor in his eyes.

She cleared her throat. ''Cord,'' she began, but she
suddenly forgot what she had been going to say. In
her confusion, she felt herself beginning to blush.

''Yes?''

*You were going to offer the use of your refrigerator,*
said a voice. It was a Spanish-accented voice, and she
thought of the priest in the dining hall. She looked

around wildly, expecting to see him peeking out from behind a bale of hay or hiding behind the tack-room door, but there was no one present other than Cord. Unless you could count the gray stable cat, which sat in a shaft of sunlight and stared at her with unblinking yellow eyes.

*The refrigerator!* prompted the voice.

Brooke drew a deep breath. "I—well, if you'd like to use the refrigerator in my place, I wouldn't mind. I can close the door between the kitchen and living room if I want privacy." Her eyes followed the cat, which got up and waddled over to a pile of empty feed sacks, her sides rounded with her pregnancy. The cat sat down on the feed sacks and began to wash her paws.

"Sure you won't mind if I use the fridge?" Cord asked.

"I'm sure."

"Maybe it's not such a good idea," he said.

She shifted her weight from one foot to the other. She hadn't expected him to back away from the offer.

"I don't mind."

Cord moved closer, his eyes dark in the dim stable light. His tone was low, almost intimate. "You know, Brooke, you shouldn't have anything to do with me. I don't always behave the way I ought to, and I'm not the kind of guy most women want to get involved with."

"I only asked if you wanted to use my refrigerator," she pointed out testily. "I don't have any hidden agenda."

He studied her face for a long time. "But how do

you know that *I* don't?'' he said. He brushed past her and strode toward his apartment. He opened the door and went inside, slamming it behind him.

Brooke stood where he had left her, her heart beating wildly. One of the horses poked its nose over the top of the stall door and looked at her with interest. In Cord's apartment, the lights flicked on, and she pictured him inside, cooking something for supper.

He'd never said for sure that he was going to take her up on her offer about the refrigerator. Should she leave the door between their apartments unlocked tonight in case he wanted to use the fridge?

Maybe she ought to have left things as they were. For a moment, she waited to hear the now-familiar Spanish-accented voice say, *You did the right thing,* but when she really needed reassurance, she heard nothing.

Except for the meowing of the cat, which, finished with her ablutions, trotted over and rubbed against her legs.

''When are you going to have those kittens, hmm?'' Brooke asked as she bent to pet her, but the cat only purred loudly. ''Looks like it'll be pretty soon.''

Well, the cat didn't seem to mind being pregnant. Maybe, Brooke thought hopefully, she'd eventually get to that point, too.

## *Padre Luís Thinks*

Foolishness, foolishness, nothing but foolishness! This woman, Brooke, she is afraid to be a mother. Can she not see that motherhood is a woman's most exalted position?

Cord wants to apologize for his thoughts. He was thinking that her problems were unimportant, and now he sees otherwise. At least Cord understands that a baby is precious, a baby is special, and each one must be treasured.

This Brooke, she comes to Rancho Encantado to learn. Perhaps I, a humble priest, will be able to help her not just to learn but to know. That is my mission, but I must do as God directs. The place now known as Desert Rose is built on the land where my hospital once stood, the hospital where I cared for the broken bodies of the people who lived here. Miners, laborers, farmers, ranchers and so many children—all were helped in my day. Now the hospital no longer exists, nor does my church or my school. But still I am directed to heal those who come to this valley, and so I shall. Perhaps it is more important to heal spirits than bodies, and that I can do. *If* the people will listen, and that is the difficulty. Most people do not listen, will not listen! I do not know if Brooke hears me or not.

Brooke does not listen yet, but she is a writer. This, I believe, means that she will heed the written word. So where can I write? On the wind? In the sky? In the dirt at my feet?

God will provide in due time. Time, after all, is all I have. Time, time, endless time…time to reflect, time to heal and help.

But Brooke does not have so much time. I must pray that I find a way to help her before she leaves this blessed place.

# Chapter Four

Brooke did leave the door unlocked between the apartments that night, pointedly shooting the bolt back so it made a loud noise that Cord couldn't help but hear if he was awake. Then she went to bed, where she slept fitfully, waking every now and then with uneasy thoughts dancing through her head of her baby-to-be. Would it be a boy? Would it look like Leo? Or maybe it would be a girl.

*It will be a beautiful baby girl.* Brooke immediately startled awake and sat up in bed, looking around to see if someone had entered her bedroom. Her first thought was that the intruder must be Cord, but she had closed and locked the bedroom door, and the window was locked, also. Still, it was almost as if the voice spoke right beside her ear. The priest again? She was too tired to think about it.

Uneasily, she fell asleep, and awoke later than she had intended. She skipped breakfast due to her unsettled stomach, and as soon as she was dressed, she headed for the Big House. There, Justine, who was talking on the phone, waved her toward the long gallery at one end of the living room. After picking her way through such leftover wedding paraphernalia as a garland-entwined arch and several tall candle stands, which were being carried out one by one by a noisy crew of cleanup folks, Brooke was pleasantly surprised when she discovered the wide array of books. She began to browse for titles that would give her a handle on this part of the California desert.

She found a couple of large volumes about the geology of the area. There seemed to be nothing, however, about the lost legend of Rancho Encantado or Padre Luís. Nor were there any books on the Tyson party or the Cedrella Pass incident.

Soon, Justine bustled out of her office, followed by a scruffy yellow dog.

"Who's your friend?" Brooke asked her.

Justine snapped a leash on the dog's collar. "This is Murphy, former cattle dog turned house pet."

Brooke bent to scratch him behind his ears, which he seemed to appreciate, judging from his wide smile and lolling tongue. "He's adorable," she said.

Justine laughed. "I don't know about that, but he's good company. Are you finding everything you need?"

"The books look helpful, but do you have any information about the legend, the ghost or the Cedrella Pass incident?"

Justine wrinkled her forehead. "As for the ghost, I've never seen him, and the legend seems to be truly lost. No one around here remembers what it was, though lots of people recall that there actually was one. It had something to do with a curse and all those people who died at the pass.''

''And the Tyson party? Are there any books about them?''

''Not that I know about. I'm sorry I can't be more helpful.''

''That's all right,'' Brooke told her. She paused. ''I don't suppose there's anyone available to show me around the Seven Springs area, someone who is an old-timer here and knows a bit about history. I'd be happy to pay for a guide.''

''I don't mind your having a look. Let me think about who, okay? I'd better take Murphy for his walk.''

''Have fun,'' Brooke told them.

After a few more minutes of browsing, Brooke departed with the two books she had found. She liked Justine, and she liked the place. She didn't think there was anything special about the ranch, unless you could count mountains that shaded from buff to lavender to deep blue over the course of the day, or sunsets that fairly took your breath away, or—well, it was an attractive bit of scenery. That was all, she reminded herself. Nothing special. Maybe that was the slant she would give the lead of her article for *Fling*.

Later, after marking some chapters in the books she'd found that morning, she had herself checked out on Stilts. The gelding was spirited, but she handled him well. After Sal gave her the go-ahead, she turned the horse toward the outbuildings in the distance near the old adobe hacienda.

Stilts proceeded at a trot along a narrow road, sandy

and rutted. Horseback was the easy way to travel in this part of the country, and she thought about the Forty-niners on their way to finding their fortunes in the goldfields. They'd had horses, mules and oxen, but even so the terrain and the climate had been inhospitable in the extreme.

The hacienda was now a private residence for the newlyweds, Hank and Erica, but there were several other outbuildings that she could explore. One seemed to be an equipment shed. When she got there, she dismounted and looped the reins over Stilts's head so he could graze on the dusty grass nearby. She approached the shed cautiously, unwilling to disturb any desert wildlife that might be camping there. The door squeaked as she opened it, and the light inside was dim.

The only inhabitants seemed to be a few spiders. After she rubbed a hole in the grime on the window with the edge of her shirt, she saw that the shed contained several old humpbacked trunks.

The locks were stiff, but she figured out how to wedge a handy crowbar under a trunk lid, and soon she had pried it open. The trunk held papers and photographs, and she sat down happily, eager to sift through them and find out what they were.

BECAUSE OF VARIOUS and sundry matters that required his attention during the day, Cord was exhausted by the time he got in that night. At the moment, the only thing that appealed to him was a large can of stew he could empty into a bowl and heat in the microwave.

He ate as much of the stew as he could, then listened for a moment at the connecting door to Brooke's apartment. He didn't hear her moving around in there. Maybe she had gone over to the rec hall, where some of the guests liked to hang out in the evening. Which meant that he could slip into her place, stash the remaining stew in the refrigerator and be gone. He was too frugal after a lifetime of hard knocks to toss out perfectly good food.

He turned the knob quietly and opened the door. The kitchen was illuminated only by the range light, and the door to the living room was closed. He didn't think anything of it, and since Brooke wasn't there, he didn't try to be quiet.

He had set the bowl of stew inside the refrigerator and was considering taking some ice cubes back to his place, when he heard Brooke's voice.

"Cord? Is that you?"

He froze, then said. "It's me, all right."

The living-room door swung open. Brooke was wearing a lightweight sweater that accentuated the blue of her eyes, and behind her he saw that the couch was scattered with papers and photographs.

"I'm working but could use a break," she said.

"Looks like you're busy," he said. He was sorry for being abrupt with her earlier, and he wanted to make amends.

"Justine said I could look through the outbuildings, where she stored a lot of old things, and I found a treasure trove." He liked the way her enthusiasm sparkled in her eyes when she talked about her work.

"How will that stuff come in handy for your article for *Fling?*" He couldn't imagine that any of the items stored in the old outbuildings would be pertinent to the trivial articles usually published in *Fling*.

"I'm working on other projects, as well. Not for *Fling*," she added hastily when he registered a dubious expression.

"Want to tell me about it?"

"I can't really say, since I'm not exactly sure where I'm going with all this. I don't suppose you'd like to see some of it."

"I, well, I wouldn't mind." He hadn't intended to visit with her. But now that he was actually in her presence, he wasn't eager to take himself out of it.

She indicated that he should follow her into the living room. "I'm piecing together who the people in some of the photographs are. Check this one." She shoved the picture across the table as he sat down on a chair.

He knew the subjects of the photo right away. "These people are Dan and Betsy Iverson," Cord said. "They were the original homesteaders here back in 1910."

"You seem to know something about this place."

"Not much."

"How about the ghost priest? What do you know about him?"

"You're asking the wrong person," he told her.

"You've never seen his ghost?"

"I sure haven't. Some people claim to have seen something, but I suspect they merely have good imaginations. His full name was Padre Luís Reyes de Santiago, by the way. There's a plaque honoring him near the place his house once stood."

"I'd like to go see it."

"It's not much."

"Could I ride there?"

"No reason why not. It's on the riding-trail map." He had an idea from the way she was looking at him that she expected him to offer to take her, but no way. He had too much to do around the ranch before he went on vacation. His vacation would be busier yet, what with trying to finish all the work at Jornada Ranch so that he wouldn't have to turn away any more boys like Brandon. He was still smarting over his conversation with Judge Ted Petty.

Brooke got up and went to the desk in the alcove. She came back with a map. "Would you mind showing me how to get to Padre Luís's place?"

He opened the map and traced the trail with a forefinger. "The bronze marker is right here," he said, pointing to where the creek divided the ranch property from the area of the desert known as the Devil's Picnic Ground. Brooke looked over his shoulder, and he could feel her warm breath on the back of his neck. He wished she wouldn't stand so close; not that he minded, but it was hard to concentrate on the business of the map with her standing so close and while he was breathing the faint scent of her soap or shampoo or perfume. Whatever it was, it smelled wonderful, like wildflowers in springtime, and it messed with his head.

In order to distract himself, he glanced away. His gaze fell on the scarred leather pouch.

She noticed that he was looking and went around to the other side of the table, thank goodness. She opened the pouch and removed two parchment scrolls. "I can't read these, can you?" she asked, passing them over to him.

He took them from her with relief, since this afforded him something to do. He understood some Spanish, but the writing on the scrolls was fancy and the vocabulary beyond him.

"What are you going to do with these?" he asked her. The scrolls seemed quite old.

"Think about them for a while, I guess. Study them. There's also an old diary."

"Would you be interested in the natural history of the desert?" He didn't know he was going to say this until the words were out of his mouth.

"I would. Are you an authority on the subject?"

"Me? No, but I have some books."

"May I see them?" She looked eager.

"If you like," he said. "Would you like to take a look through my bookcase?"

He stood up and handed the scrolls back to her. "I'll go poke around the apartment and see what else I can turn up. Come over when you're ready."

"I'll only be a minute."

*Sheesh,* he thought. *I was going to turn in early in preparation for the things I need to do tomorrow, but now that won't be possible.*

For a moment he regretted being so helpful, but then he decided that he didn't mind all that much. Brooke was a distraction, and not an unwelcome one. He only wished he didn't have the idea that she liked him way too much for her own good.

BROOKE DIDN'T RUSH to get ready to go over to Cord's, mostly because she wanted to give him time to neaten things up if that was what he wanted to do. After she smoothed her hair and put on a fresh coat of lipstick, she went through the open door to his place.

His kitchen was neat, but she saw no personal touches. Cord hailed her from the living room, which seemed sparsely furnished. There was a tall bookcase beside the couch, and an enormous chair that had seen better days. He had a small television set, and no curtains hung at the window. Still, the place seemed to suit him—no nonsense and no frills, very much like Cord McCall himself.

After browsing through the bookcase, she chose some titles about the plants and animals of the desert, and Cord brought her another about mining operations. "Do you mind if I take them over to my place?"

"No, of course not."

She noticed that his name was neatly written in the front of each book. Clearly, this was a man who prized his books and took good care of them.

"How did you come by your interest in these things?" she asked, thumbing through the volumes she'd chosen.

He turned away, suddenly busy. "Grew up here," he said.

"You grew up at Rancho Encantado?"

"No. Nearby. My father worked in mines here and there."

She was accustomed to interviewing subjects for articles, and the signs were unmistakable: this was a topic that Cord didn't want her to pursue. But that had never stopped her before, and it didn't stop her now.

"So your interest is personal?"

"Maybe." He rose from his position in front of the bookcase. "You know, I really need to get some shut-eye. Big day tomorrow."

She turned to go, walked through the kitchen. He followed along.

"Thanks, Cord. You've given me a lot to go on."

"Don't mention it." He held the door open for her.

"See you tomorrow," she said. She closed the door, but after a moment's thought, she didn't bolt it.

"YOU SAID YOU GOT these books from Cord Mc-Call?" asked Bridget, the twitchy little clerk in the office.

Brooke waited while the photocopy machine spit out another copy. "Some of them. Justine gave me the rest."

Bridget was studying the dust jacket of a book that Brooke had set on her desk. "Looks halfway interesting, I'd say. I can't imagine Cord McCall reading any of these," and she gestured at the other books spread out on the table beside the copier.

"Why is that?"

Bridget shrugged. "He doesn't seem the type to sit home at night and read books."

"He has an extensive collection," Brooke replied, checking the copier to see if it needed paper.

"You've been in his apartment?" This question was delivered with an expression of pure incredulity.

"Just for a few minutes last night."

"Oh, my, I do believe you're the only person who has ever been invited inside."

This caught Brooke's attention. "What's wrong—is Cord particularly antisocial?"

Bridget snickered. "He shows up at the ranch square dances on Friday nights by order of Justine, but he never stays long. He usually cuts out and, well, I'm not going to tell you where we think he goes." She shuffled a stack of papers and dropped them into a file folder, looking busier than she actually was.

"You mean Miss Kitti-Kat's?" Brooke asked ingenuously.

She was rewarded when Bridget's jaw dropped. "It didn't take long for you to find that out," she said.

"Mmm," Brooke replied.

"The question is, is it really true that he goes there? That's what nobody knows."

Brooke picked up the book she'd been copying and slammed it shut. "I'd say that's Cord's business, wouldn't you?"

"Oh, of course," Bridget replied hastily. Before long, she disappeared into the back room and sat down at her computer, the urge to gossip apparently stilled.

Brooke smiled to herself as she left. Somehow, she had become Cord's champion, his advocate, which she thought entirely unnecessary. Cord McCall looked able to take care of himself. Yet there was no way he could protect himself from gossip, she supposed, though he seemed unconcerned about what anyone might think of him.

In that way, she supposed, they were much alike. She didn't care what anyone thought about her bearing this baby and keeping it. The difference was that no one was talking about her, because, aside from Leo, no one knew about the baby except Cord.

That would soon have to change, but not yet.

CORD SPENT another restless night. In the morning he was reminded of why he'd slept so poorly when he woke up and saw the empty spaces in his bookshelf. He prized all his books, every one. He hadn't been able to enjoy the luxury of books when he'd been rodeoing, or at least books that he could keep. Yet most likely, it wasn't the absence of his books that bothered him. It was the presence of Brooke last night in his small apartment.

He spent most of the morning going over ranch accounts with Justine, who had in the past proved that she could be his biggest fan or greatest detractor. They had just finished their work and he was gathering up his paperwork to leave, when Justine casually mentioned that she had invited a freelance writer to stay at the ranch while working on an article about the place.

"That would be Brooke, right?"

Justine's head snapped around. "I thought I saw you two talking at Hank's wedding," she said with a knowing look. What it meant exactly, Cord wasn't sure.

"Right," he answered. He opted for a quick change of subject. "Do you want me to phone those figures to you here at the Big House or e-mail them before I go on vacation?"

"E-mail is fine, but could you consider postponing your vacation?"

He was blindsided by the request. "Postpone my vacation? I scheduled it a month ago!"

"Has it ever occurred to you, Cord, that you've taken quite enough time off as it is? That you probably owe me time, not vice versa?" Justine eyed him sternly.

"Damn," he muttered.

"Look, Cord, I've been ignoring your frequent disappearances because you're the best ranch manager I've ever had. It so happens that the situation has changed since you told me you wanted a week off. I've got two guys sick today—no telling when they'll be back to work. Another quit this morning, that fellow from Arizona, and there's the new hire, Pearsall, to train. I've got to worry about cows giving birth and getting cattle to auction and—well, you know the drill."

"I know it all right," Cord said stiffly.

"And now here's this writer, this Brooke Hollister. She has the potential to give us some great publicity. I'm worried about the health spa and dude ranch end of the business, Cord. Client reservations are down for this summer, probably because of the economic situation."

Cord wasn't sure what he was supposed to reply to this. His responsibility was the working ranch, not the dude ranch-health spa operation that Justine prized so highly. After a moment's consideration, he settled on a mildly interested, "Is that so?"

"*Fling* is the most popular magazine for young

women on the West Coast, and it would be great if we could increase our clientele in that age group. Plus, Brooke might be able to place other articles about Rancho Encantado in more far-reaching publications.''

"I fail to see what that has to do with me."

Justine narrowed her eyes at him. "You've become friendly with her. You're bound to see each other going in and out of your apartments. I think you're just the one to take her under his wing at Rancho Encantado."

Cord knew that his employer's impatience was exhausted. He hadn't been a model employee since he'd bought Jornada Ranch and commenced with the repairs to it. Sometimes things went wrong there and he had to put them to rights; sometimes he bugged out of Rancho Encantado, thinking no one would miss him, that no one would be the wiser. Well, apparently that hadn't always been true.

Justine went on talking. "Cord, weren't you born around here?"

"Well, yes."

"And raised here?"

"Sure," he said reluctantly.

"I want you to make Brooke Hollister a priority. Take her where she wants to go, be available whenever. You'll get a bonus from me for any extra time you put in, and as for your usual recreational pursuits, putting them aside for a couple of weeks if I make it worth your while wouldn't hurt you."

He was only a month or so away from quitting this job altogether. Telling Justine what she could do with the job and how he felt about being ordered around was on the tip of his tongue. But he respected the woman; he couldn't help it. And if he quit now, he would have less money available to spend on the kids who needed it.

"Think you can handle it, McCall?"

The way Justine spit out those words sparked a willingness to show her he could handle anything she tossed his way. "I think so," he said, biting his own words off sharply.

Justine afforded him an abrupt nod. "Great. I don't think looking after Brooke will qualify as hard duty, by the way. She's quite attractive."

He managed a grunt, and then someone came to the door and he made his escape. All the way back to his apartment, he seethed. Like he needed something else to do right now. Like he wanted to give up his "usual recreational pursuits," which almost made him laugh. Apparently, Justine had bought into the prevailing rumor that he hung out at Miss Kitti-Kat's.

Cord's phone was ringing off the hook when he stopped by his apartment to drop off the paperwork. He only hoped it wasn't Ted Petty again. He was still frustrated that he hadn't been able to help the boy Ted had told him about.

It wasn't Ted. It was Mattie, his right hand at Jornada Ranch. "Cord, Cord, there's a mistake. I thought I'd better call right away."

He was accustomed to Mattie's dire outlook. "Now, Mattie, calm down. What's the problem?" He leaned back against the wall, prepared for a long, involved story. Mattie couldn't help it; she didn't know how to abbreviate.

"The shingles for the bunkhouse roof arrived and they're the wrong color! They don't match the sample you showed me. The man who drove the truck is related to my cousin who lives near Beatty. He said he was told to bring the shingles. The roofers will be here any minute. I sure can't let them put these shingles on the roof if they're the wrong color!"

Mattie, bless her heart, was a conscientious worker, and that was why he employed her. If it wasn't for this job, she'd be hard-pressed to survive, since she was also supporting her lone grandchild, a five-year-old boy.

"Hold on, Mattie, dear. What color are the shingles that were delivered?"

"Brown. You wanted gray. The color of the shingles is to blend in with the desert, you said. You said—"

"Never mind what I said. I meant to tell you that I changed the order to brown. You can let the roofers have their way with the roof. Don't let them have their way with you, though, Mattie. I'm counting on you to remain faithful to me."

"Oh, you, Cord. You big tease. I'm beyond all that silly business."

She was a good soul, and she liked his teasing, despite her protestations to the contrary. "You're my favorite girlfriend, and don't you forget it." Mattie was seventy if she was a day, and she was crippled with arthritis. The illness had made it impossible for her to continue her work as a seamstress at Rancho Encantado, where she'd been employed for many years.

"How could I forget I'm your girlfriend? You never let me." A clamor arose in the background, and Cord grinned into the phone.

"Is that Jonathan? Let me speak to him."

A rustle, a laugh, and then Jonathan came on the line. "Cord, Cord! When are you coming to see me?"

"Soon, Jonathan. Are you behaving yourself?"

"Oh, yes. I helped Granny make the beds today. I'm learning to clean the windows. Granny sprays the blue stuff on, and I wipe. I'm good at wiping, Granny says so."

"That's great, Jonny. Let me talk to your granny again," he said.

Mattie came back on. "Cord, you take it easy. You are too busy, much too busy." She'd adopted a scolding tone.

"You shouldn't give me such a rough time," he said.

"Thank goodness you will be here all next week on vacation."

"Uh, Mattie. The plan has changed. I can't take my vacation now. It has to wait."

"Wait? But you promised you'd be here next week!"

"Justine has other plans for me."

"You work too hard, Cord. If you weren't working so hard, you wouldn't have forgotten to tell me about the change in the color of the shingles."

"You'll agree there's no harm done, right? I'll take my vacation soon. You know I want to finish up at Jornada Ranch as soon as possible. Bear with me, Mattie. Don't quit on me now."

"I'm not only your best girlfriend, I am your biggest fan. You're going to make a difference in the world, Cord, and I'm proud to help."

"Thanks, Mattie. I'll get over there and see to things as soon as I can manage a few hours away."

"Jonathan and I miss you very much," Mattie said.

When he hung up, Cord had to pull himself back to matters at hand. He had to remind himself of all the things he needed to do. E-mail those figures to Justine, find out if Hank had ordered enough feed for the stable horses before he left, find out why the refrigerator repairman still hadn't shown up.

And figure out how he was going to usher Brooke around Rancho Encantado and environs without wanting to jump her bones.

# Chapter Five

*There is nothing special about Rancho Encantado.*

Brooke stared at the letters on her laptop screen and chewed on her lower lip. This was supposed to be the lead for the *Fling* article, but the words weren't coming easily today.

She got up, went to get a can of root beer, and leaned against the kitchen counter to drink it. She attributed her difficulty with the lead to the research she was pursuing for the book she wanted to write. She'd begun reading the old diary to see if it could possibly have been written by Annabel Privette, her great-great-great-grandmother, but she'd soon discovered that the author was someone named Jerusha Taggart.

She picked up the diary from the kitchen table and leafed through it, stopping to read a few of the entries, not in any particular order.

October 25, 1849
    This was a grueling day requiring much walking. Nathan cried all morning and fell asleep in

the wagon afterward. I checked him for fever and
thankfully found none. I pray to God that we survive this cruel desert.

Brooke knew that she would have to start reading
at the beginning of the journal to learn who Nathan
was and even who Jerusha was, though from some of
the subsequent entries, she gathered that Jerusha was
Nathan's mother. Carefully turning the pages so that
they wouldn't fall apart in her hands, she went to the
beginning and started reading again.

July 15, 1849
I'm optimistic about California, where my husband says we'll find our fortune. Dear Teensy can
hardly contain her excitement now that we have
almost reached Santa Fe. I am as excited as she
but must remain calm for the sake of my family,
which, God willing, will soon be larger. I've not
mentioned my suspicion to my dear husband, as
it would only worry him.

Who was Teensy? Dog? Child? It was hard to tell.
As for the growth of Jerusha's family, she must mean
that she was pregnant and keeping the news from her
husband.

The sight through the kitchen window of Cord
McCall striding into the stable interrupted Brooke's
thoughts. His hat was pulled down over his forehead
and he carried a sheaf of papers.

She couldn't decipher the expression on his face,

but she decided that there would be no better time to ask him if she could keep his books awhile longer.

She stepped outside the kitchen door. "Cord," she called. "Do you need those books back right away?"

He looked at her as if he hadn't expected to see her standing there, and she had the idea that his thoughts were miles away. "No, you can keep them for a while."

"Thanks." She paused. "By the way, I didn't get to Padre Luís's place today. I found something interesting, though."

He looked her up and down with a hint of impatience. She suspected that he objected to her taking up his time with trivialities.

"Yeah?"

"The diary I found seems to be that of a young woman who was with the Tyson party."

This made a heat flare in his eyes, or was it only her imagination?

"I'm going to read the rest of the journal, find out who she was."

"Great."

She turned to go back in her apartment. Suddenly, there was a shuffle and Cord cleared his throat. "Justine says I'm to take you anywhere you want to go. She says I'm in charge of you."

"In charge of me?" She pivoted and stared.

"That's what she says." Brooke could tell he wasn't too happy about this state of affairs.

"Well," she said slowly and consideringly. "I didn't ask for that."

He studied her face. "No, I don't suppose you did."

"I'll try not to be too demanding."

He took off his hat and ran a hand through his hair. "Where would you like to go? What would you like to do?"

"I'm not sure yet. I'm just getting into this."

"Maybe we could go into town and grab something to eat while we kick around the possibilities," he said.

This was a surprise, considering that he hadn't seemed to want to linger. "Okay," she said cautiously. "Where would we go?"

"There's only one place, the Lucky Buck Saloon. It's run by a local guy who recently moved back from Texas, and until lately the only decent food was pizza. Joe's recently added sandwiches to the menu, and they're not bad."

This sounded better than listening to gossip in the communal dining hall. "Come on in. It'll take me only a few minutes to get ready."

When she emerged, Cord looked her up and down. She'd put on her suede jacket, which was a shade of dusty coral, and she'd pinned her hair back from her face. His scrutiny made her feel self-conscious, though, and she busied herself checking her purse for lipstick, wallet and credit cards.

"My car or yours?"

"We'll take my pickup," he said as he followed her out.

She climbed into the truck and tried to untangle the seat belt, which was looped over itself in a way that made it impossible to fasten. She wasn't able to straighten it out by the time they reached the entrance to the property, the pillars supporting the sign that said

Rancho Encantado, Where Dreams Come True. Cord had been observing her without comment as she tried to figure out how to make the belt work, but all of a sudden he braked and pulled over to the side of the road.

"Here," he said, "let me help you. Hasn't been anybody riding on that side of this truck for a while." He turned slightly to face her and set to work, his big hands working the belt this way and that.

"Now," he said when he had finished. "Let's see if this works." He reached for the belt's clasp and pulled the belt taut across her abdomen. Her first concern was of the new life that she harbored there, but her second was that having his hands near that part of her anatomy was much too intimate, too threatening. And yet she didn't feel threatened, not at all. Overshadowing those thoughts was another one: that she would soon be adjusting seat belts to accommodate her increased girth. Or maybe pregnant women didn't wear seat belts. Did they? She couldn't remember what any of her pregnant friends had done, but surely they wore their belts to protect both them and the baby. Well, she realized with a start, she certainly had a lot to learn about pregnancy, motherhood and babies.

"All right," Cord said, jamming the truck into gear and pulling back onto the tarmac. "Off we go to town. Have you been through Sonoco yet?"

She refocused her thoughts. "No, I drove here from L.A."

"Of course. That means you'd be coming from the other direction. Well, Sonoco isn't much of a place. It's way down on the list of fashionable spots."

"It's a former mining town, right?"

"They once hauled a lot of copper out of the hills near there. Now it's not exactly a ghost town, but the miners have gone. It's on a highway, so there's a lot of through traffic."

They had pulled onto that highway only a few minutes ago, and looming on her side of the road was a large billboard. Miss Kitti-Kat's Teahouse, it said. A well-endowed cartoon cat winked and blinked alluringly at passersby.

She edged a glance over at Cord. He didn't seem to notice the sign. He drove at a speed well over the limit, and though Brooke was aware that many drivers sped on these long, straight desert roads, there was a hint of recklessness in the cant of his strong jaw, the careless way in which he gripped the wheel. She had the feeling that he would welcome the truck's spinning out of control so that he could wrest the vehicle from danger, that he would take great satisfaction in doing so.

As they left the valley, the desert stretched in all directions, pushing the mountains toward the horizon. It was a sere landscape yet eerily beautiful, and Brooke shivered when she thought about how forbidding it must have appeared to the people who were destined to cross it by wagon train in the days of the California gold rush.

In the distance, a whirl of dust was kicked into motion by the wind, and she leaned forward in her seat to see it better.

Cord noticed. "Dust devil," he said succinctly.

"A dust devil? What's that?"

"Some of the Indians around here think that their ancestors' spirits live on in the dust devils." The dust looked as ephemeral as smoke as it took on a life of its own above the desert floor.

"Nice story, but what are they really?" The dust devil resembled a midget tornado.

Cord shifted in his seat and narrowed his eyes briefly at the dust devil before returning his gaze to the road. "When the wind hits an obstacle, like a rock, it can start the air spinning. As the air carries the dust upward, a vacuum forms in the center and more air rushes in to fill the vacuum. That's how a dust devil fuels itself."

This particular dust devil seemed to grow in velocity as they watched, merrily wending its way through clumps of creosote and sagebrush.

"What's the speed of the wind in one of those things?"

Cord shrugged. "They say it reaches up to fifty miles an hour within the cone."

"I'd like to see one up close," she said.

"We can do that," he said, and before she knew it, he had swerved the pickup off the road and onto the desert floor and they were bumping and lurching over rocks and ruts.

Brooke laughed in amazement. She gripped the armrests and held on for dear life, since Cord didn't seem in mind to slow down anytime soon. He gunned the pickup across a dry wash, laughing right along with her.

"I didn't think you'd actually chase this thing," she shouted.

He slanted her a reckless look. "You said you wanted to see one up close. Don't say it if you don't mean it!" he shouted back, and then they were almost level with the dust devil, and then they were in it, in a maelstrom of dust and leaves and debris that sizzled grittily on metal and windshield.

Brooke felt a peculiar light-headedness, a dizziness. For a moment she thought she was being caught up in the dust devil, but the notion was so absurd, sitting as she was in a perfectly sturdy pickup with all four of its wheels touching the ground, that she dismissed the idea immediately. But as she watched, the whirling leaves and dust formed themselves into— Her name? The letters B R O O K E? It was impossible. She was seeing things. She blinked once and whatever she'd seen was gone, was again nothing but a bunch of wind-driven debris.

And then they were out of it, leaving the swirling wind behind with their exhaust. She twisted around in her seat to stare at the dust devil, half expecting to see the letters of her name in its midst. But no, she didn't.

Cord slowed the truck and grinned at her. She stopped hanging on for dear life and, the strange mirage momentarily forgotten, she grinned back.

"Did you enjoy that?" he asked.

"Yes! But…" Her voice trailed off. She didn't think Cord had seen what she had. Nor had *she* seen it, probably. It must have been an optical illusion or something.

"But?" He was looking at her questioningly.

She decided not to mention the letters of her name. He'd get the idea that she was bonkers or worse. "Um,

our little adventure certainly made me forget my
queasy stomach,'' she said, settling back in her seat.

A contrite expression washed over Cord's features.
''I'm sorry. I didn't think.'' He slowed the truck to a
sedate speed and picked a way clear of stones, ruts
and boulders to get them back on the highway.

''No, I'm fine,'' she reassured him. ''I liked it.''

''I wouldn't have pegged you for a lady with a
sense of adventure.''

''You would have been wrong,'' she said.

''I see that.''

She grinned at him, wishing she felt comfortable
telling him about the repeated sightings of Padre Luís
and now the illusion in the middle of the dust devil.
She didn't understand what was going on, and she was
reluctant to discuss any of it with Cord.

She was quiet as Cord drove the rest of the way to
Sonoco, and he didn't speak, either. As they approached the huddle of buildings that soon appeared
on the horizon she sat forward in her seat.

Even though she knew that Sonoco was a small
town, she was still surprised that the main street was
only two blocks long. The only businesses were a gas
station, a small grocery and the Lucky Buck Saloon.
A few streets wandered off the main drag into the hills
and were lined with mobile homes. The more pros-
perous-looking of these had dusty trucks hunkered
alongside.

The building housing Miss Kitti-Kat's was the
town's largest structure and was situated at the end of
one of the streets. Painted mustard yellow and identified by a large roof sign bearing the same picture of

a winking bejeweled cartoon cat that Brooke had seen on the billboard earlier, it would be hard to miss if you happened to be driving through.

Brooke ignored the place, and although she watched Cord curiously for some reaction, he seemed oblivious. They drove past the gas station and pulled into a parking lot beside the Lucky Buck, a small brick building with a false front. It was surrounded by cars, many of them with out-of-state license tags.

Inside, the sound of slot machines provided the only music. Cord led her to a booth along the back wall and grinned apologetically. "Sorry about the ambience or lack of it. That's the way it is."

A stocky man with a mustache stuck his head out of the kitchen as they sat down in a booth. "Hey, Bucky," he said. "Be with you in a minute."

"Take your time, Joe."

"What did he call you?" she asked curiously.

"An old childhood nickname." Cord's face had gone still, and he picked up a menu and began to study it.

"You don't seem to like it much."

He spared her a quick look. "Bucky, shortened from Buckaroo. I don't like to be called that."

"Oh, okay. Lots of people don't like their nicknames."

The proprietor came over with an order pad. Cord introduced her to Joe, who asked, "What can I get for you?"

"A chicken sandwich for me."

"I'll have pizza."

"It'll be right out." Joe hurried back into the kitchen.

In the booth behind Cord, a young couple with a child who appeared to be about eighteen months old were finishing their pizza. They had released the little girl from her booster chair, and she stood on the seat, peering over the back of the booth. Her eyes were wide and brown, and she had soft reddish curls falling across her forehead. Brooke thought she would like it if her baby looked like this one, then chided herself. Babies came in several different models and sizes, no one better than the other.

"Careful, Lindsay," the mother said, but she and the father were figuring the bill and didn't make the baby sit down. Lindsay, the baby, reached out and touched one finger to Cord's cheek.

He turned around. "Hey there," he said softly. "Who are you?"

"Me me me," said the little girl.

"Well, you you you, you're mighty cute."

The child's mother smiled. "This is Lindsay," she said. "Is she bothering you?"

"Not at all," Cord answered firmly, and Lindsay beamed.

The father and mother resumed counting out money to pay their check, and Cord swiveled slightly so he could see Lindsay better. "You want to see my mouse?" he asked her.

Lindsay nodded solemnly, and only then did Brooke notice that Cord's hands had been hard at work. Slowly, he raised the paper napkin that he had ingeniously wrapped around two fingers and fashioned into a mouse shape, complete with a twisted paper tail.

"You have to be careful about mice," he told Lindsay as he wiggled the napkin across the seat and up the back. Spellbound, she didn't take her eyes off the mouse. It reached the top of the seat back and twitched there for a few moments.

"My mouse just woke up," Cord said. "My mouse is looking for a little girl named Lindsay."

The girl's gaze went from the mouse to Cord's face and back again. "My mouse wants to find Lindsay," Cord said, moving the napkin mouse closer to Lindsay with every word. "And he has!" With that, he slid the mouse up Lindsay's arm to the side of her neck. Lindsay giggled wildly, and her mother and father joined in the laughter.

"Come on, Lindsay. It's time to go." Her father slid out of the booth and lifted her in his arms.

Lindsay wrinkled her forehead and held her hands out toward Cord. "Mouf? Mouf?"

Cord slid the play mouse off his fingers. "Here, you'd better take the mouse with you," he said to the parents. They thanked him and set off toward the front of the restaurant, disappearing down a row of shiny slot machines.

After they had left, Cord turned back around. Brooke had been surprised by his enthusiastic entertainment of the little girl; she would not have expected Cord McCall to like children.

"Why are you looking at me like that?" he demanded.

"I was surprised that you were so good with that baby."

"Kids like me," he said.

"I see that. I wouldn't have expected it."

"Am I that bad? That forbidding?"

"I didn't say forbidding."

"Kids—they're special. They come into this world through no wish of their own, and they're totally innocent and unmarked. They deserve adults in their lives who care about them."

These words were delivered with such vehemence that Brooke, who had been toying with the paper wrapper from her straw, looked up sharply. Before she thought of a reply, Joe brought their food, and she busied herself with salting her sandwich. When she bit into it, she was surprised at how good it tasted; either that, or she was unusually hungry after not eating much all day. This train of thought reminded her why she wasn't often hungry these days: the baby. Her baby. Who might resemble little Lindsay but more likely would not. She honestly didn't care what the baby looked like. Imagining it was hard, that was all and maybe she was clutching at whatever she could to personalize the new little life inside her. If she could picture it, if she could imagine it, perhaps she could begin to have welcoming feelings for it.

Cord cleared his throat. "I hope you didn't take all that stuff I said personally."

She didn't know what he meant. "What stuff?"

"About kids. You've been so quiet that I thought maybe I've offended you. When I said that they come into this world through no wish of their own, maybe you thought I meant your baby. I didn't.''

"I suspected that you were generalizing."

"I was, sort of." He shifted in his seat. "We're not here to talk about personal things, Brooke. Suppose you help me out and tell me what you need to know about Rancho Encantado."

The light in his eyes was sincere enough. She took heart from this and plunged ahead. "As of now, I'd like to know about the lost legend. Why the place is supposed to be so special. What the deal is with the vortex." She ticked them off one by one on her fingers.

"You want a lot," he said.

"Maybe, so let's focus on the lost legend for now."

"There's no way to focus. It's lost."

"What do you know about it?"

"Very little."

"You're not going to tell me."

"What's to tell? There is a legend. No one remembers it. It was probably a lot of hooey, anyway." He forked a giant piece of pizza into his mouth.

"Well, I'm pretty sure by now that you're not the Rancho Encantado publicity flack," she said despairingly.

He narrowed his eyes. "Do I detect a bit of dissatisfaction here?"

"I thought," she said with as much patience as she could muster, "that you were appointed to help me."

"I get it," he said. "You're going to report me to Justine."

"Did I say that?" She thought maybe he was joking.

"You don't need to."

"Look, I don't rat on anyone. Got that?"

"Right." He said it as if he didn't believe it.

"Okay, so you can't tell me anything about the legend. How about the vortex?"

He started to chuckle. "Like I know anything about that. Oh, I've heard the word bandied about among the guests here, but all I know is that it's some New Age blather."

"I heard some guests talking about energy centers and negative ions," she said. "They said Rancho Encantado's a special place."

"It's a special place only because it's in a green valley located in the middle of a big desert," Cord said. "All the other stuff is just—stuff."

"Oh, Cord," she said, "how can you say that when so many people obviously believe?"

"People believe in the tooth fairy, too, but do you?"

She couldn't help laughing. "Yes, I do. My father was quite a generous tooth fairy in his day."

"That was lucky." He was back to that stiff manner that he always displayed when conversation veered in certain directions—namely, family, childhood or home.

"You didn't have a good tooth fairy at your house?" she asked.

"No."

She waited to see if he would elaborate, and the silence stretched long between them.

"I didn't have any tooth fairy in my whole life," he said finally.

"I'm sorry, Cord," she said quietly.

"Yeah, well, you and a lot of other people."

He had a chip on his shoulder, one that must be too heavy to carry most of the time. Yet she sensed that he might want to unburden himself.

"Are your parents still alive, Cord?" she asked gently. Her sandwich forgotten, she studied his face. The scar gave it character and interest, and suddenly, she found herself captivated by the finely honed edge of his chin. Or was it the groove on his upper lip, or the sexy droop of his eyelids at the corners? She looked away, her mouth dry with what she recognized as sexual attraction. But how could she be lusting after anyone in that way? To feel sexual attraction when you were pregnant wasn't possible, or was it?

Cord didn't seem to notice her unease. "My father is dead. I never knew my mother."

Brooke made herself stop thinking about her attraction to this man and thought, instead, about her mother, so caring and kind. All of a sudden, she remembered the tooth pillow that her mother had made for her out of white satin. It had been shaped like a large molar. There had been a little pocket on the front for the tooth, and the pocket was big enough to hold a couple of bills from the tooth fairy. Her father, so patient and hardworking, still farmed the same plot of land that had been in his family for three generations. There seemed nothing to say to Cord but, "I'm sorry things were difficult for you, Cord."

"It all happened a long time ago," he said, but there

was a world-weariness to his voice that, in that moment, made him seem older than he looked. She found herself hoping he would enlighten her further, but his expression was shuttered now, and she had the feeling that nothing she could say would make him open up.

He called to Joe and ordered a beer. "Want anything?" he asked her.

She shook her head. She was searching for some suitable topic, one that wouldn't make him uncomfortable, when he said suddenly, "When did you say your baby's due?"

Grateful for the lifeline, she didn't even mind that it was a question that only a couple of days ago she would have considered too personal. "In October. The nineteenth, if I calculated correctly."

He nodded. "October is a nice month to be born. The weather's cool, and if you live in the climate for it, there's fall color."

"And Halloween," she said. "I can use a Halloween theme for birthday parties."

"Candy corn. Costumes."

She smiled. Then she sobered quickly. "I can't imagine this baby being big enough to wear a costume. I wish I could. I wish the baby were more real to me, but right now it's only a strip of paper from the pregnancy test that turned the wrong color."

He cocked his head. "You're kidding."

"I don't know any babies, Cord. How can I imagine mine?"

"You'd better start," he said.

"Isn't it a little premature? I've got six months, after all."

"Brooke, it's important for you to start bonding with this kid. You're its mother. You're the most important person in the world to your baby."

"I know that," she said unhappily. "I liked the baby that we just saw—Lindsay. She was cute. I didn't hold her, though. I didn't feel her weight in my arms. What do babies smell like, for instance? I haven't a clue."

Cord stared at her for a long moment, and as if he had suddenly had an idea, he stood up. "Come on, Brooke. We're leaving."

"You haven't finished your beer!"

"This is more urgent."

She glanced at the rest of her sandwich. She wasn't all that hungry anymore. Still, she didn't understand what he had in mind.

"Let's go." After she slid out of the booth, he took her arm.

"Where are we going?" she asked as he dragged her through the cloud of cigarette smoke that surrounded the slot machines, which kept ringing and zinging and, in the case of one bespectacled matron, spitting out coins.

"We're going to go look at Exhibit A."

"What *are* you talking about?"

"Brooke, this evening you are going to meet a real-life, perfectly charming, extremely delightful baby, who is Exhibit A in the Preparing for Parenthood course."

They burst out into the clean cool night air. She

shook his hand off her arm and stood stock-still in the parking lot. "Wh-what?"

"A baby, Brooke. Didn't you understand what I said? I'm taking you to meet a baby."

## Padre Luís Speaks

I am but a poor priest, and it is not easy. I still cannot imagine what possessed someone to give the former site of my hospital a name like Desert Rose and then place a cactus garden in the middle of the courtyard! I was blessed with a sense of humor, but this does not seem funny to me.

Brooke needs help, like so many others who come here. Too often the people who travel to this blessed site suffer from sicknesses of the soul. It is my given mission to assist all who come here, with God's help. And who am I to question why I am the instrument of God? I am a poor priest, but also a humble one, not to mention confused.

Why am I confused? I was for some time confined to my cactus patch and unable to move about. Now I am no longer required to stay there. I can go where I will. So, in the spirit of helpfulness, I showed myself to Brooke in the place where everyone eats. Did she see me? I do not believe so. I have spoken into her ear when she needs guidance. Did she hear me? *Madre de Dios,* I think not.

You know, when I worked with Erica, who married Hank, I lost my voice for a time. The cat had got my tongue. Yes! It happened! I do not know why. I do not question. But now that I can leave my cactus patch, now that I have my voice back, I am frustrated that Brooke cannot see or hear me. What am I to do? How am I to reach her?

Brooke is with child. I can feel the heaviness of her soul resting upon my shoulders. I am thinking, how do I communicate with Brooke? She is a writer. She understands the written word. Thus, I must write. I tried it today. I wrote Brooke's name upon the wind. The wind sailed away across the desert and was caught by a dust devil, a jolly little fellow. I do not think that Brooke was able to see the message. As for the dust devil, he has gone on to bedevil somewhere else.

I must think. I am thinking. Hmm…

I have it! Brooke has a strange book in her room. It has keys with letters on it, and when she taps the keys she makes words. The words appear magically on the screen of this book. ¡Madre de Dios! Perhaps I can do this.

The strength of my God is everywhere. Now I ask him to grant this poor priest a favor and allow me to reach Brooke through this magical book in her quarters.

With God's help, all is possible. I must pray that my favor is granted.

*Chapter Six*

Cord pulled the pickup to a stop outside a small neat house with a baby stroller on the front porch.

"Where are we?" asked Brooke. She looked disconcerted, which wasn't so surprising. He had refused to answer any of her questions on the ride from Sonoco to Rancho Encantado.

"This is where my friends Dusty and Tanya Smith live." He slid out of the truck and hurried around to open Brooke's door. He helped her down from the seat, deciding that he needed to be more mindful of her condition. She wasn't going to be a mother; she already was, albeit an expectant one. Considering the importance of her need to accept her new status, he'd better remember that.

"Do they know we're coming?"

"No, but they won't mind if we stop by. You might have seen them at the wedding. They brought their baby but left before the reception so they could put her to bed."

The curtained windows in the front of the house gave off a warm golden glow, and while they waited for someone to answer Cord's knock, Brooke had a chance to study his profile. It was a strong one, the nose long, cheekbones high and sturdy, chin like a rock. And then there was that scar, faint now in the light beaming from the windows.

The door swung open to reveal a woman who was about Brooke's age. "Why, Cord," she said, sounding pleasantly surprised. "It's good to see you."

"I've brought someone to visit, Tanya. I hope it's not too late."

"Of course not." She called over her shoulder. "Dusty, Cord is here, and he's brought a friend."

A slim man hurried out of the kitchen, carrying a baby. "Cord, what's up?" He handed the baby to his wife and shook Cord's hand.

Cord made introductions all around. "Dusty is ranch foreman, second-in-command of the cattle operation. Tanya is a stay-at-home mom. And this is Emma," he said as the baby stared at both of them.

They stepped into a cheerful room furnished in soft blues and pale yellows and were invited to sit in the living room. "Brooke is a freelance writer who frequently has articles in *Fling* magazine," he told the Smiths.

"I love that magazine," Tanya said. She set Emma on the floor, and the baby toddled across the living room toward them. She was a pretty child, with curly dark hair and blue eyes. Those eyes sparkled up at them as she wrapped her arms around one of Cord's legs.

Cord reached down and swung her into his arms. Emma smiled and patted his face. "I haven't see you in a while," he said. "You're getting to be a big girl." He set her back on the floor when she struggled to get down.

"Emma will be a year old next week," Dusty said. He sat down beside his wife and casually slipped an arm around her shoulders.

"How about a piece of blueberry pie? I baked it today," Tanya said.

"I bet it's good, but none for me. Brooke?"

Brooke shook her head, her gaze remaining fixed on Emma, who had made her way across the floor and was now handing toys to her mother. Tanya accepted them one by one, her lap growing full.

"I brought Brooke here because she is interested in babies," Cord said.

Dusty laughed. "You're in the right place," he said.

"Oh, am I going to be quoted in *Fling?* I'd like that!" Tanya seemed thrilled.

Brooke shot him a look that said, "Now what?" but she didn't correct Tanya's misconception that she was writing an article about babies.

Emma bent to pick up a fistful of toys, then tottered over to a wastebasket and dumped them in, chortling all the while. "She must be a handful," Brooke observed curiously. Were all babies in constant motion like this one? How would she work at home if she was tempted to play with a baby?

"She's a very busy child now that she walks."

"Do they usually start walking so young?"

"Some do, some don't. Emma took her first steps a few weeks ago at ten months, so she's an early walker."

"Ten months!" Brooke hadn't thought that babies could walk when they were so young.

"I had a nephew who walked at eight months," Dusty said.

Emma made for Brooke's purse, which she had placed on the floor beside the couch. Brooke snatched it away, worried that Emma might trip over the strap.

Dusty came and picked up his daughter, planting a kiss on her cheek. "No, no, sweetheart. That doesn't belong to you." He put her back down. "Where's your rubber duck?" Tanya held out the toy, and Emma made a beeline for it. She immediately stuck its head in her mouth, dropped to her hands and knees and began to crawl rapidly toward the kitchen.

Brooke watched all of this with fascination. "Does Emma still nap?"

"Oh, yes, every afternoon, but she had a late nap today, so she's unusually wide-awake this evening."

"But they sleep a lot when they're little, right?" She didn't see how she'd be able to get any work done if her baby didn't start out sleeping most of the time.

Tanya chased Emma into the kitchen and brought her back to the living room, where she sat in Tanya's lap. "It is true they sleep most of the time at first, waking to be fed or have their diapers changed." She laughed. "I like being an authority on babies. What else would you like to know?"

"I'd like to learn more about their first three months," said Brooke, feeling that Tanya would be able to see right through this ruse and wishing that Cord had never put her in this position.

"You know, Brooke, I think I have something that

will help you. I saved a bunch of publications from the pediatrician's office, and if you'll excuse me, I'll sort through them to see if we have any extras.''

"If it's not any trouble," Brooke told her.

"It's no trouble at all, but it will take a few minutes." By this time, Cord and Dusty were discussing ranch matters, and Tanya brought Emma to Brooke and deposited her in Brooke's arms. "I'll be right back."

Brooke stared at Emma. Emma stared back. Then she blew a bubble and grinned.

The men paused in their conversation. "I think Emma likes you," said Dusty.

"I hope so," Brooke said. She stared dubiously at the baby. "There are so many things that can go wrong with a child this age. I'd be afraid to leave her for even a minute."

"We have a baby monitor," Dusty said. "It takes some of the worry out of being a parent."

"A baby monitor? What's that?"

Dusty grinned. "A year ago I'd never heard of one, either. It's an intercom device that helps you keep tabs on a baby in another room of the house."

"Obviously, there's more to bringing up a baby than I ever thought," she said soberly. "Baby monitors. Who would have guessed?"

Tanya returned from the back of the house, carrying a handful of pamphlets. "These will fill you in on a lot of the basics," she told Brooke as she gave the booklets to her. She swung Emma up into her arms. "It's time for this little one to go to bed," she said. "Say good-night, Emma."

What Emma said didn't sound remotely like "good night," but her goodbye wave was enthusiastic and completely understandable. Tanya bore her away, and Cord wound up his discussion with Dusty.

"We need to be going," Cord said. "I've got a full day tomorrow."

Tanya called out her goodbye from the back of the house, and Dusty walked them to the door.

"Thanks," Brooke said, feeling guilty that she wasn't really writing an article about babies.

"Anytime," Dusty said.

When they were walking to Cord's pickup, Brooke glanced over at him. "They're a nice family," she said.

He looked pensive for a moment. "That's true," he said. His face was silvered by starlight, his eyes shadowed and dark. He slid a glance in her direction. "Was Tanya helpful?"

"I may have questions I want to ask her once I've read the pamphlets." She felt wistful as she was struck with the realization of how much her life had changed; before she and Leo had broken up, before she was expecting a baby, she would have been planning romantic weekend trips to the Napa Valley wine country, not collecting pamphlets about child care.

They got in the truck, and Cord started it. He slowly drove the short distance back to the stable and pulled up in the parking area alongside the corral.

Cord didn't switch the ignition off. Instead, he turned to her. "I'm going to drop you off here before I go check on the newborn calves."

"Can't I go with you?"

He stared in surprise. "Do you really want to?"

"I, well, I'm suddenly interested in babies. Of all kinds."

"There's a heap of difference between a calf and a human baby," Cord said dryly, but he shifted into reverse and began to back out of the parking space. They didn't have to drive far, and as they climbed out of the truck near the calving shed, someone hailed Cord from the barn.

"I'd better see what Vernon wants," he said.

"Take your time," Brooke told him.

As Cord strode off, Brooke continued to the shed, buttoning her jacket against a chill wind that was whipping down out of the western mountain. The building had a Dutch door, the top part of which had been left open. Inside, illuminated by the light of a low-wattage bulb, were several cows, one lying in the hay. That one scrambled up when she saw Brooke's face and backed into a corner, nearly trampling her own calf.

"Hey! Don't go in yet!" Cord was headed toward the shed on a run.

Brooke wheeled in a panic. "I'm afraid that cow is going to hurt her baby."

"Hey, Daisy! Move it," he said to the cow. And to Brooke, "She's a little scared right now, that's all. A cow tends to get right protective when she's got a new calf."

At that point, the cow snorted and stomped in their direction. "Simmer down there," Cord said to the cow, which only glowered at him.

"I'll go in, see what's what," he said. "Vernon

mentioned that this one gave birth late this afternoon. Looks like a pretty calf, too.'' He opened the door and entered cautiously, talking soothingly to the angry cow.

She lowered her head, calmer now, and nosed her calf, which now lay in the straw. The calf seemed alert, and after Cord spoke to the cow for a while, she allowed him to check her baby over.

''That's a fine calf, Daisy,'' he told the cow. ''A nice addition to our herd.''

Cord let himself out the door and joined Brooke in leaning over the door's bottom half to observe.

''Sorry about Daisy over there,'' he said, inclining his head toward the now-docile cow. ''Cows that are new mothers perceive people as a threat sometimes, and she doesn't know you.''

''It's natural to want to protect one's young,'' Brooke said thoughtfully. As a mother-to-be, she wanted to keep her child safe from harm, too. She didn't have to love her baby in order to protect it.

But she wanted to love this baby. And she didn't yet.

She turned away so that Cord wouldn't see her distress. She had been on an emotional roller coaster almost from the instant of conception. She'd gone through a lot in the past couple of months—breaking up with Leo, realizing that he didn't share her dreams of a life together, forcing herself to face the fact that he was never coming back. Then she'd found out she was going to have his baby, and even though she had been in denial about it for the first few weeks, she'd thought she'd accepted the pregnancy. She hadn't, though. There were layers upon layers of motherhood that she hadn't considered yet, and each time she uncovered a new one, it hit her hard.

"Ready to head back?"

Although she was still grappling with her new and overwhelming emotions, she nodded and followed Cord to his pickup. When they arrived at the stable, he stopped the truck and said, "What about tomorrow? Is there anything you want to see?"

To think about this with thoughts of motherhood swirling in her head was difficult. She slid down from the seat before replying. "I want to ride up to Cedrella Pass."

Cord shook his head slowly. "You shouldn't attempt it on horseback. It's too far."

"It doesn't look so far on the map."

"Once you cross the salt flats and get into the mountains, it's mostly up and down. The only way to get there and back in one day is to take a four-wheel-drive vehicle."

"Oh." Disappointment flooded her.

"Besides, Brooke, that's not an outing you should tackle alone."

"Why not?"

"The pass is too remote, and it would be easy for you to lose your way. Why don't you explore closer to home—wouldn't you rather see the old borax mine? Or check out some of the sights around the desert?"

"I'm more interested in the Tyson Trail and the people who suffered at Cedrella Pass." She started walking toward the stable, her suede jacket flapping in the wind.

"You don't want to go there, Brooke."

She sighed, then turned around at the stable door and waited for him. "You're the one who doesn't. Never mind." Maybe she could find a guide in Sonoco. There must be people who would take her to Cedrella Pass for a fee.

"What's the big attraction, anyway? I don't get it at all."

"I want to research the history of this area."

"That doesn't seem to fit in with the type of article they publish in *Fling*."

"The research is for another project that I might want to pursue someday. Anyway, what's your problem with history? I should think you'd be in favor of my learning more about the area."

"Not that history," he muttered. The words were scarcely audible.

She glanced over at his stony profile as they resumed walking. "Something's bugging you. I wish you'd tell me what it is."

"When Justine said I was supposed to squire you around, she didn't mention anything about Cedrella Pass, that's all."

"I didn't say anything to her about going there."

"I suppose Justine will have a fit if I don't take you."

"Oh. Well, in that case, what time tomorrow do you want to leave?"

He gazed off into the night, at the mountain range in the distance. Deep in its shadows lay Cedrella Pass and the Tyson Trail. He heaved a sigh. "The earlier the better."

"Before dawn?" She started up the steps to her door and turned when she reached the top one. Since she was a good deal shorter than he was and was standing on the top step, her face was a little higher than his. She noticed that he had to tip his head back to look her in the eye.

He rested one boot on the lower step. "We could leave around seven," he said.

"In your truck?"

"I'll borrow Stumpy's Jeep. It's a better off-road vehicle."

"Fine. Knock on the connecting door when you're ready. Better yet, come over and have coffee with me."

He appeared startled at the suggestion, and she had the fleeting thought that maybe not too many people knew him well enough to offer simple friendship.

"That's not necessary," he said.

"I know."

He shifted uneasily and removed his foot from the step. "I told you I'm not the kind of guy you want to get involved with."

She heaved a sigh of impatience. "Look, Cord, it was only a simple invitation."

"All right. Coffee in the morning. I take mine black."

"Fine. I'll call the kitchen and ask them to provide a picnic lunch." They could pick it up before they left.

"See you tomorrow," he said, his voice slightly this side of gruff and sounding rusty.

"Great. I'm looking forward to going to Cedrella Pass."

He didn't say that he was, but she didn't mind. He reached up and, gravely courteous, tipped his hat to her before opening his door and going into his own place.

Bemused by their whole exchange, Brooke stepped inside her apartment, switching on lights as she hurried to her desk. It was still early, so she sat down and turned on her computer. She needed to get to work, but somehow Leo and Felice and *Fling* and the promised interview with Malcolm Jeffords seemed far, far away and not important in the scheme of her life. What was important was this baby she was going to have, and learning to love it, and learning to love—yikes! She had almost added Cord McCall's name to that list.

The only importance he had in her life, she reminded herself sternly, was to provide information. But in a flash of insight she acknowledged that she could remind herself of his unimportance as often she liked, the hard part was making herself believe it.

THE DAY HAD BEEN A LONG ONE, and Cord was more than ready to hit the sack. But tonight his double bed looked too big for one person and far too lonely. As he went around straightening things in his apartment, he forced himself to stop thinking about the lush curve of Brooke's lips, the gentle sweep of her neck above her collar. He reminded himself that she was going to have a baby. Soon, her body would be swollen with pregnancy, heavier and rounder by far. She would have that ripe, glowing look that was so attractive in women who were about to have a child. At least, he found it attractive. Pregnancy gave women a certain voluptuousness that they couldn't attain otherwise.

He heard the wood floor creaking next door as Brooke moved around the apartment. He couldn't help wondering how long it would take her to settle down and get to bed. Would she jump in a shower? Wash her hair? Eat a snack? He flashed on her first day here, when he'd surprised her by trespassing in her apartment and had found her in bed nearly naked. He'd seen her nipples through the thin sheet—big brown ones, the kind he liked best, the kind that he'd bet would harden and tighten at the slightest touch. He ached to touch them—and all of the rest of her.

Never mind how long it would be until Brooke went to bed; for him, it would be a while. With the image of her still emblazoned on the inside of his eyelids, he headed to the bathroom for a shower. A very cold one.

BROOKE, sitting at her computer, stared at the line she had written that morning.

*There is nothing special about Rancho Encantado.*

Her lead still hadn't led into anything. She didn't know enough about Rancho Encantado to proceed. That could be because she hadn't done a lot of the things that clients were urged to do. The oasis hot pool, for instance. According to the Rancho Encantado registration literature, the natural rock-lined hot tub, located in the date-palm grove was fed by one of the hot springs in the area. She ought to go there.

But not tonight. She was still too keyed up over the evening, still thinking about Cord. Who would have known that the man liked babies? Who would have dreamed that he was so thoughtful? She recalled the determined look on his face as they drove from the restaurant in Sonoco to the Smiths' home. And then there was his patience with the cow and her calf. He had been so caring, so unruffled. He seemed like a gentle man.

*There is nothing special about Rancho Encantado, except Cord McCall.*

She stared at the words. Had she actually typed that last part? Oddly enough, she had no recollection of doing so. She stared so long in disbelief that the words grew blurry on the screen. And then, she saw other words faintly inscribed behind those that she had written. She had never seen anything like them before— pale, almost indecipherable lines of print.

She reached for her reading glasses and perched them on the end of her nose. Leaning forward, she peered through the lenses at the screen of her laptop. The faint lines behind her words wavered and glimmered, making them impossible to read.

"Computers!" she exclaimed. "It's always something." Like, needing to install a new memory card last month. Like, having her printer repaired only a week ago. Of course she hadn't typed that part about Cord McCall. It was a computer error. A glitch.

By this time she was so sleepy that she could hardly keep her eyes open. That was pregnancy for you, she reminded herself with resignation. There was no point in trying to work when she felt so tired, so she put on her nightgown and crawled into bed. She thought about Cord, whose bed would be on the other side of this wall. Tentatively, she placed her palm against the wall, wondering if he might be doing the same thing. The wall felt warm, and for a moment she had the sensation that the barrier had disappeared and Cord was reaching out to her from his bed, touching her hand, twining his fingers between hers.

It seemed so real, his touch. In fact, in that instant she believed that she could guide his hand to her breast, curve it around the contours rounded with pregnancy, and that his hand was cool against the heat of her nipple. But it was only fantasy, only a wish.

Yet this was Rancho Encantado, Where Dreams Come True. Would *her* dream come true? No. It wasn't a dream that she had any business having.

She yanked her hand away and turned over, putting her back to the wall. Still, maybe if she listened carefully, she might hear the creak of bedsprings on the other side.

But she heard nothing, because she immediately fell asleep.

# Chapter Seven

Late that night, the strident ringing of the telephone woke Cord from a deep sleep. He groped for the phone, elbowing himself up against the headboard of the bed and wincing at the pain that always accompanied his waking. The red numerals of the digital clock indicated that it was five in the morning.

"Cord! Cord!" It sounded like Jonathan.

"Jonny?"

"Cord, I remember you said that if I needed to talk to you, I should push the button on the phone."

"What's wrong, Jonathan?" Cord had programmed their phone to dial his number when someone punched the button next to his picture. This must be an emergency.

Fully awake now, Cord ran possible scenarios through his head. Mattie had fallen and hit her head. Mattie had gone outside and not come back. Lots of things could happen to a woman her age who suffered from high blood pressure and arthritis.

"I heard something, Cord. I heard a noise."

"What kind of noise, son?"

"Like—like a thump."

"Where is your granny now?"

"She went in the bathroom. I talked to her. She won't come out."

"All right, Jonathan. Take the phone with you and go knock on the bathroom door. I want to talk to your granny." He was already sliding his T-shirt over his head. He had left his jeans on the closet floor, and, moving stiffly, he went to get them.

As he struggled to pull them on with only one hand, he heard rustling on the other end of the line, then voices. In a few moments Mattie picked up the phone.

"Mattie? What the hell is going on?"

"Oh, Cord, it's nothing. I woke up early and couldn't go back to sleep, so I got up to go to the bathroom and ran into the chair I moved yesterday."

She sounded sleepy, not to mention annoyed. He couldn't figure out if she was glossing over something serious or telling the truth.

"What chair?"

"That rocker that used to be in the living room. I moved it into the bedroom earlier today so I could sit beside the reading lamp next to the bed while I let out the hems of Jonathan's dress pants. He's growing so fast, you know."

Cord supposed this story made sense, but as an ex-seamstress, Mattie had an area set up in the unused dining room where she usually did her sewing. That is, when her fingers weren't too swollen to prevent her from using a needle and thread.

"You ran into the chair and woke Jonathan?" The boy slept in the bedroom next to Mattie's.

"Apparently. I told him I'd be right out of the bathroom, but he called you anyway."

"Cord *said* to," Jonathan piped up in the background. "He said."

"Put him on, Mattie, please."

Mattie handed the phone over, and he heard Jonathan say anxiously to her, "Am I in trouble, Granny? For calling Cord in the night?"

Cord hastened to reassure him. "No, Jonny, you are not in trouble. I'm glad you called. I want you to be my eyes and ears at Jornada Ranch."

"Okay, Cord. I will."

Jonathan handed the phone to Mattie, and Cord said to her sternly, "I think you should move that chair back where you got it."

"All right, Cord. When are you coming over here?"

"Today," he said. He slid his keys across the dresser before pocketing them.

"So soon!"

"Yeah. I'll see you in a bit."

He wanted to get over there and reassure himself that she was really all right. It had been almost a week since he'd made an appearance, and that was too long.

After he was in his truck and rolling toward the highway, he remembered with a start that he was supposed to take Brooke to Cedrella Pass in the morning. Well, they could leave a little later than they had intended, that was all.

It was still dark out, and there were few other cars on the highway. This gave him plenty of time to think, and what he thought was that it would be pleasant to have Brooke riding along beside him, watching the first pale fingers of dawn reach up from the mountain range in the east.

BROOKE ROSE around six-thirty that morning and started the coffeemaker before she jumped in the shower. She put the butter out to soften before she plugged in the toaster, and she set two mugs on the counter. The fragrant aroma of coffee filled the air, and she wondered if Cord could smell it in his apartment. As she toweled herself dry, she listened to see if she could hear him next door. It was quiet over there…too quiet.

While she was putting on makeup, she thought about the strange dream she'd had last night. Something about the priest, Father Luís. She'd dreamed that she'd read a message from him on the screen of her laptop computer, something about someone who was going to help her. Oh, well, that would be Cord—no big shocker there. But she felt uneasy about the dream nonetheless.

Her uneasiness disappeared during a moment of true despair while she was dressing. Her jeans wouldn't snap. She was gaining weight already, and she thought she detected a slight change in the contour of her abdomen. Sighing, she pulled the bottom of her turtleneck out of the jeans and left the snap unbuttoned underneath, but her despair faded as she began to anticipate seeing Cord today. Somehow, he made her forget the things that were wrong with her life and reminded her of the things that were good. She needed to be reminded of those things, and often.

In the kitchen, she was suddenly overtaken by a

wave of nausea, which abated almost as suddenly as it had arrived. All right, she thought. No coffee and no breakfast for her this morning. Instead, she nibbled on saltines and glanced at the clock. It was six forty-five.

She still heard no sounds coming from Cord's apartment, which was odd considering that they had agreed upon seven o'clock for coffee. She went to the connecting door and listened for a few moments, and when she realized that no one was moving around on the other side, she called, "Cord?"

There was no answer, so she knocked, and then she knocked again more loudly. Nothing. No one.

She opened the door. "Cord, are you here?"

By this time, it was clear that he wasn't. She hadn't heard him leave in the middle of the night; not that she necessarily would have, but she sometimes heard his door opening and closing when he came in or went out. Acting on a hunch, she hurried to the window and checked for Cord's truck.

It was gone.

She moved away from the window, bewildered. They'd made a date. She had been counting on his showing her Cedrella Pass, and he'd agreed, albeit reluctantly. Disappointment washed over her, followed quickly by anger.

Knowing that she was intruding and sure that Cord wouldn't approve, she walked slowly through his shadowed apartment, taking note of the unmade bed in his bedroom. The last time she had seen that bed, on the night he'd given her the books to read, it had been neatly covered by a quilted bedspread. If Cord had gone out last night, wouldn't the bed still be made? Of course, she didn't know if he made his bed every day. Some people didn't.

Perhaps there was an emergency somewhere on the ranch and his presence was required. But why wouldn't he have left her a note? Or called her to let her know? He presumably knew how to use a telephone.

Maybe there was no emergency at all. Maybe he had gone to Miss Kitti-Kat's. That was one of the options, Brooke figured. Certainly, that was what the local gossips would want everyone to believe.

Cord had convinced her that she couldn't go to Cedrella Pass by herself. It was probably too late to hire someone to take her there. With a crushing sense of letdown, she realized that she'd have to find something else to do today. Underlying her disappointment was her indignation at being stood up.

She was seething by the time she left the apartment. When she next saw Mr. Cord McCall, she'd give him a piece of her mind.


WHEN CORD ARRIVED at Jornada Ranch, it was barely light out. Jonathan was watching TV in the big living room and eating dry Cheerios from a bowl. Cord let himself in quietly, but as soon as Jonathan spotted him, the boy bade him an enthusiastic welcome.

"Cord! I knew you'd come! I've missed you!"

He picked the boy up and tossed him into the air. "How's the man of the house, huh?"

Jonathan's dark eyes sparkled. "I'm fine. Granny's fine. At least, I think so. She's in the utility room."

"Let me check with her, and then I'll come back and watch TV with you for a while."

Jonathan returned to the cartoon on the screen, while Cord went through the kitchen to the utility room.

"Mattie?"

He saw her slumped in a chair beside the washing machine and rushed to her side. She looked up in surprise and started to rise when she heard his footsteps. Her hair, steel gray now, framed a face that sagged with fatigue. She had on a rumpled housecoat, not her usual immaculate slacks and shirt, and she wasn't wearing lipstick. He didn't think he had ever seen her without it.

Cord didn't like the look of her. "Mattie, don't get up. What's wrong?"

She eased back on the chair and forced a smile, and in that smile he could see vestiges of the pretty woman she had been long ago. "Nothing is wrong, Cord. I decided to sit down for a few minutes before I took the clothes out of the dryer is all."

"You don't look so good, Mattie." Dark circles rimmed her eyes.

Mattie summoned up a sparkle. "Is that any way to talk to your favorite girl?" With some effort, she pushed herself up from the chair and opened the dryer. She began to pull clothes out and drop them into a basket on the floor.

Cord sat down on the chair. "If you aren't well, you should tell me. I'll hire someone to help you." She had an infinite number of nieces and nephews who could be pressed into service if necessary.

Mattie shot him a playful glance. "Help me? Don't be silly. Jonathan and I can handle any business that arises just fine, thanks."

He couldn't have accomplished nearly as much without Mattie to take care of things. Due to her help, he had been able to keep his Rancho Encantado job and renovate Jornada Ranch at the same time.

She was looking a bit sprier now that she was folding laundry. Maybe he should give her the benefit of the doubt. "All right, Mattie. If you're really okay, I'll go take a gander at the new roof."

"You do that. Then you'd better focus your attention to the bunkhouse. Pack rats have built a nest in there again."

He'd dealt with pack rats before. They were a big nuisance in the desert, and they were hard to dissuade. He'd better get rid of them as soon as possible, because he needed the place habitable. Then he could get the state licensing agency's seal of approval and welcome his first guests. He sure didn't want to turn away any more boys like Brandon.

"Before I get rid of the pack rats, I'll spend some time with Jonathan," he told Mattie. He became aware of the aroma of coffee wafting in from the kitchen. "Mind if I help myself to a cup of hot brew?" He felt a stab of guilt about Brooke. He'd better give her a call from here and attempt some explanation, though he couldn't get too explicit without telling her where he was, and such was his habit of secrecy that he didn't want to do that.

"You go right ahead and make yourself comfortable. You know where I keep the cups.'' Mattie added a pair of neatly folded overalls to the stack.

Once he had a hot mug of coffee in hand, Cord dialed the number that he knew by heart from when Hank had lived in the apartment that Brooke now occupied. The phone rang and rang, but she didn't answer. This didn't surprise Cord. By this hour the spa would have opened and she was probably availing herself of some of Rancho Encantado's well-touted amenities. He tried calling her several more times, but she still didn't answer. He wished she would. He knew now that he wouldn't make it back that morning; there was too much that needed to be done around here.

''Cord? Do you want to play Mr. Mouth?'' Cord had given him the game for Christmas.

''In a minute,'' Cord said, grabbing a couple of Mattie's homemade biscuits from the platter on the counter. They were slightly stale. She must have made them yesterday. That in itself was significant; she'd always whipped up a fresh batch as soon as she arose, which was customarily at an early hour.

''I'll go get the Mr. Mouth game,'' Jonathan said.

Cord went and sat down in the living room, not too interested in the zany cartoon characters on the TV screen but willing to put up with them for Jonathan's sake. He would have rather been talking on the phone to Brooke. He still didn't know how he was going to explain why rushing away so early in the morning had been important, but he'd think of something.

AFTER SHE REALIZED that Cord wasn't going to show, Brooke went over to the spa and managed to wangle an appointment for a massage. She not only had a wonderful massage, but foot reflexology and aromatherapy, as well. Somewhere along the way, her morning sickness disappeared, so she considered the massage time well spent.

Afterward, while her bones still felt pleasantly liquid, she almost bumped smack into Joanna Traywick. The doctor had been having a massage in the adjacent cubicle.

"Aren't you looking fit!" Joanna exclaimed.

"I should be. That masseuse really knows how to get the knots out."

Joanna laughed. "I feel ten years younger myself. Say, how about stopping at the juice bar with me? I hear they serve a mean glass of carrot juice."

The juice bar was in a sunny, wide-windowed room overlooking the palm grove. They perched on high stools and drank tall drinks from frosty glasses—carrot juice for Joanna and papaya for Brooke.

"I've heard that papaya juice settles the stomach," Brooke said after her first sip. "Do you think there's any truth to that?"

"Possibly." Joanna paused for a none-too-subtle assessment. "I know it's none of my business, but maybe I can help if you're having stomach problems."

Brooke smiled ruefully. Joanna had been friendly, and hers was the type of personality that inspired confidences. "I'm pregnant," she admitted, feeling shy about saying the words. This was only the second time she'd uttered them; maybe the more often she told people, the more she'd actually believe it herself.

Joanna nodded knowingly. "I thought it might be possible," she said carefully.

Brooke blinked. "You did?"

"There's something—well, incandescent—about pregnant women. And then there's the matter of the dream I had the night you arrived. It was so vivid that it woke me."

"What kind of dream?"

"About a priest in the cactus patch at Desert Rose. I think it was Padre Luís, the one who built the school and hospital here in the valley. He said your name and pretended to rock a baby in his arms. I got the idea. My medical specialty is obstetrics." She laughed. "I have to admit that a cactus patch is not exactly where you'd expect to see a priest, and he certainly didn't say what you'd expect a priest to say if you *did* see one."

Brooke remained silent for a moment. "Are you sure it wasn't a ghost?"

Joanna shook her head. "Who knows? At the time, I decided that the dream was probably the effect of hearing too many rumors about this place and not getting enough sleep. I had a hard time becoming accustomed to the quiet here in the desert, and the first few nights I tossed and turned a lot."

"Not me. I've slept very well. Pregnancy does that to a person, I guess."

"I know. That's what my patients tell me."

"Joanna, since you're an obstetrician, I have some questions for you. Like, how soon do I need to start having prenatal checkups? And when will this morning sickness end? And why am I always so tired?"

"You should find a good obstetrician as soon as possible. Prenatal care is important for both you and your baby," Joanna replied. She went on to offer a prescription for a safe antinausea medication and to reassure Brooke that her unusual fatigue was normal in the early months.

"I can't thank you enough," Brooke told her when they rose to leave.

"No problem," Joanna said warmly. "Call if you need me, okay?"

After Joanna went off to her Pilates class, Brooke headed for her apartment. Cord's truck wasn't in the parking area when she got back, so she surmised that he was still away. Where he was wouldn't be any of her business, she reminded herself, if he hadn't stood her up this morning. She had wanted to see Cedrella Pass. Of course, Cord had no idea why visiting the pass was so important to her. He didn't know about her great-great-great-grandmother and how she had died there.

But perhaps Jerusha Taggart did. Carefully, so as not to crumble the thin pages of the old diary, Brooke opened it to where she had left off.

December 9, 1849
    Today one of the oxen died. Teensy cried when we told her. Nathan did not seem to care. He grows weaker each day. I walk as much as I can to save the oxen, though I am weary. The new babe in my womb has the easiest lot. Annabel has grown very thin and seems so weak. I worry about her.

Annabel! Brooke made a notation of the page. Trying not to hurry for fear that haste would make her rush past valuable information, she pored over the pages of the diary. She learned that the Tyson party had splintered off from a larger wagon train at Santa Fe, where they had encountered a former army scout named Willis Tyson. He had claimed to have a map showing a shortcut to the goldfields. Several families, eager to get across the desert with its forbidding mountains and wary of the customary northern routes because of the coming cold weather, had thrown in their lot with him.

Brooke kept reading, looking for another mention of her ancestor Annabel, this time along with her surname. That would confirm that Jerusha Taggart knew her.

Finally, she found it. On a page in the middle of the diary, Jerusha had arranged the names of the members of the Tyson wagon train in family groups. Annabel was listed under the name Privette along with her husband James and three children, Lucy, Jody and Melissa. Lucy Privette was Brooke's great-great-grandmother.

Brooke felt a thrill of discovery. She had not given much thought to her ancestor except as a member of the ill-fated party that had suffered so much hardship at Cedrella Pass. Now, as she ran her fingers across Annabel Privette's name, actually written by a woman who had known her, it was as if she felt her presence.

Abruptly, she stood up, feeling a shiver despite the warmth of the room. She would go for a walk in the hope of clearing her head.

As she emerged from the stable on the path, Brooke met Justine hurrying over from the Big House. Murphy, her dog, romped along beside her. Justine was carrying a big clipboard and looked pleased to see her.

"Hello, Brooke! I trust all is going well with your article?"

"Yes, thank you. The apartment is working out well. I think I'll stay there for the duration."

Justine smiled. "I knew you'd like it. Not only that, but as you've probably discovered by now, Cord lives right next door. I asked him to show you around and answer any questions you might have. Did he mention that?"

Brooke hesitated. "Well, yes." She didn't plan to expand on this, but Justine skewered her with a glance.

"I hope he's been helpful."

"I—um, yes, he introduced me to the ranch foreman and his wife, and he lent me some material."

Justine studied her face for a long moment. "Cord isn't here, is he?" she asked bluntly.

The last thing Brooke wanted was to get Cord in trouble. "I haven't seen him lately," she hedged.

Justine looked extremely put out. "That Cord! If I know him, he hasn't been around all day. One of the men called to ask if Cord was at the Big House this morning when they were having trouble with a cow in labor. I didn't hear from the guy again, so I assumed that Cord must have shown up. I'll bet he's off on a toot."

"Toot?"

"Off doing whatever it is that Cord does—not that he enlightens anyone. Excuse me, Brooke, I'd better get on his case." Lips clamped in disapproval, Justine headed toward the Big House, her rigid blond braid swinging angrily behind her. Murphy, after a galumphing detour through the stable, followed.

She'd gotten Cord in trouble, all right. Brooke took no satisfaction in the fact, but you'd think that if Cord valued his job here, he'd play by the rules. Which apparently included acting responsibly, not that he seemed to care.

Brooke set off toward the Smiths' small house, deciding in that moment to let Cord collect his just desserts. Since they were in the middle of a desert, that was sort of a pun, and she would have liked someone to share it with. However, that someone was nowhere to be found.

AFTER A BRIEF VISIT with Tanya and Emma, Brooke headed back toward her apartment, determined to read the pamphlets that she'd been avoiding ever since Tanya had presented them to her. Even so short a time spent around a year-old baby had convinced her that staying in her small one-bedroom apartment in L.A. would no longer be possible. Babies took up more room than she'd ever dreamed; plus, they needed equipment—playpens, baby monitors and who knew what else? She would need to see about finding someplace bigger as soon as she returned to the city.

As Brooke skirted the corral on the way toward her apartment, she spotted Cord's pickup as it barrelled into its parking place. He couldn't help seeing her, and he was out of the truck in an instant.

"Brooke!" he called. "Wait!"

For a split second or so, she didn't intend to stop walking or to alter her path. He must have thought she didn't hear him, and he called to her again.

With extreme patience, she turned in his direction. "Yes?" she said with the proper degree of chilly politeness.

"I want to explain about this morning," he said. He strode toward her, and although his step was firm, she thought he looked tired. He came to a stop in front of her, his forehead furrowed, the corners of his mouth turned down.

"I tried to call you, but you weren't in," he said.

"I waited for an hour or so before I left the apartment."

"I would have been here, but it was important."

"Important?"

"Yes. Something came up."

A vision of Miss Kitti-Kat's mustard-yellow building imposed itself on her all-too-vivid imagination. She wasn't inclined to be understanding.

"You could have left me a note."

"I should have. I apologize, Brooke. We'll go to Cedrella Pass tomorrow, I promise."

True, he looked contrite, but he offered no further explanation, and she didn't feel comfortable asking questions. If Cord McCall wanted to spend his time in a brothel, she supposed it was no concern of hers. Still, she recognized her disappointment in him. Despite the rumors, she had not believed them.

"I'll meet you in the stable at seven in the morning," she said tersely, then wheeled to go. She hadn't mentioned his dropping in for coffee, nor did she intend to.

She was surprised when he caught her shoulder. "I had something in mind to make it up to you," he said.

She whirled, surprised when her eyes met his to discover that they were serious and somber.

His hand dropped to his side. "I thought—dinner," he said, sounding much less sure of himself.

She couldn't believe this. The guy had stood her up, apologized without giving a full account of himself and now expected her to sit down to eat dinner with him? She walked to the corral, where one of the men was working to train a horse to the saddle.

She watched for a minute, then turned to Cord. "You must be kidding," she said flatly.

He'd followed her to the fence and leaned one shoulder against it. "I brought something. A friend of mine makes great chili. I have a large pot of it in the truck."

"Chili," she said. As usual since she'd become pregnant, anything spicy appealed to her.

"Do you like chili?"

"Well, I—yes."

"Good. My place or yours?"

She decided to be frank. "Why should I eat dinner with you, Cord?"

"Because you want to?"

She had always been a sucker for boyish charm, but somehow, that quality was unexpected in Cord and all the more appealing because of its contrast to his usual nature. He looked so hopeful, so comically repentant, that she couldn't stop herself from smiling. The smile became a chuckle, and the chuckle morphed into a laugh.

"Do I take this as a sign that I'm forgiven?"

"Not exactly. Take it as a sign that I like chili."

"What else could I do to make things right with you?"

"Stop trying to worm your way back into my good graces."

He grinned at her. "Have I succeeded?"

"Don't you have something you should be doing? Like, finding out about the latest emergency over at the calving shed?"

His eyebrows flew up. "What do you know about that?"

"Justine mentioned it earlier. She said you've been AWOL."

He let out a long breath. "Ah, the charming Justine. I thought I could go and return before she even noticed I was gone."

"When you've been gone since early this morning? That's quite a while, Cord, and apparently Justine doesn't miss much that goes on at Rancho Encantado. The only person you're fooling is yourself if you think your absences aren't noted."

"As we say around here, Justine rules with an iron feather."

"What do you mean, an iron feather?"

"When she's trying to prove a point, she's all fluff, but when she wallops you, you feel it."

"Sounds as if you have personal knowledge of such things."

"I've been walloped, if that's what you want to know. Did she come around looking for me?"

"One of the hands thought you might be at the Big House this morning and asked Justine where you were. Some problem with one of the cows."

"Great. Say, I'd better get that chili into your refrigerator before I check in with the guys."

"Fine." Brooke waited while he got the pot of chili and a six-pack out of his pickup and took them inside her place. When he came back out, he stopped to give some pointers to the man who was training the horse, before walking to where Brooke still stood.

"You sound like you know what you're talking about," Brooke said as they watched the horse go through its paces.

"I understand a good bit about training horses. Did it for a long time."

"Here at Rancho Encantado?"

Cord flicked his gaze in her direction. "Not here. Other places."

"Rodeos?"

"Where did you find out about that?"

"It's the scuttlebutt around here."

He leaned across the fence. "Don, try a different bridle. See if that works." He turned to Brooke.

"Yeah, I did some rodeos, made my living the hard way."

"Why did you quit?"

"Accident," he said as though he didn't want to discuss it.

She supposed that a rodeo rider eventually getting hurt was a given, and she would have liked to know more about his injury. It could explain the stiffness that she detected in the way he walked, and the pain associated with it could account for his gruffness at times.

Cord moved away from the fence as Don began to fit the new bridle on the horse. "I've got to get over to the calving shed," he said, but he appeared preoccupied, not really in the moment. He was acting as though he had something more important on his mind than what was happening here. Hanging out at Miss Kitti-Kat's shouldn't make him so distracted; maybe he had other things going on in his life. She'd had that feeling about Leo at times during their relationship, and ignoring it had been a mistake.

Thinking about Leo left a sour taste in her mouth, and she turned to go.

"Brooke?" Cord's hand was on her arm.

"I'm going back to my place. I'll see you later, okay?" She was suddenly so sleepy.

"Sure."

"And don't forget to watch out for Justine, in case she's still gunning for you."

Cord seemed to drag himself back to the moment. "What time should we have dinner? Around seven?"

She'd almost forgotten about the chili. "That's fine. Come over early. We can eat at my place."

"Great. I'll see you then."

Leaving Cord to his work, Brooke headed for her apartment. This sagging fatigue threatened to drop her in her tracks, made it hard to focus on her work. She hoped she could get in a nap before dinner.

## Padre Luís Writes

Brooke! Brooke, can you read this? I have tried so hard to reach you, but I think I have failed. Nevertheless, I must write this message in the hope that you will read it on your machine. Forgive me, for I am not a writer. I am a humble priest, trying every way I can to reach you, but I cannot make the words come up on the magic book so you may read them! I am beside myself with worry over this matter.

Child—and I hope that you do not mind my addressing you in this manner, since we are all children of God—you must continue to think of your own child as you have begun to do. Each child is a gift, and each one is special.

You believe you do not love this child yet. Love will come in due time. You must open your heart. Yes, I know that is not easy. I know that your heart is hurting because of the bad experience with the man you loved. But there will be another man for you, a better man. A man who understands the specialness of children.

I am a poor humble priest, only doing the job that is set before me. I do not question the ways of God. I only question the ways of man, which is something you are familiar with, no? You have questioned the ways of men many times. Many, many times.

I am smiling to myself. It is good that you have a questioning mind. You will find out what you need to know. This I promise you.

Now I must rest. Writing is not easy for me. If we could talk, I would ask you the nature of this magic book that you use for your work. *Por Dios,* but it is a clever sort of machine! I would like it if you would write back.

But I suppose that communication from you is too much to expect when you don't seem to know that I exist. Even I am not so sure sometimes that I exist! *Ay de mi,* this is a strange life for a priest. Perhaps I should pray.

Pray, then rest. That is a good plan. Peace be with you, dear Brooke. ¡Hasta la vista! Until later.

Your humble servant,
Luís Reyes de Santiago

# *Chapter Eight*

"The chili smells absolutely wonderful," Brooke said.

"It is," Cord assured her as he bore steaming-hot enamel bowls of food to the table. Brooke had set the table with cloth napkins and flowers. He'd asked where she'd found them, and she told him that the napkins had been in a kitchen drawer and the flowers in a trash bin behind the communal dining hall.

"Left over from the wedding, maybe," she said as she tore open a package of saltines.

"Ah, the wedding." He didn't know why he felt so bleak every time he thought about Hank and Erica's being married. He'd always considered it something of an advantage to be single, especially when he was traveling with the rodeo. He hadn't had time for serious relationships.

Brooke set the salt and pepper shakers on the table. "There," she said. She glanced at the overhead light. "I wonder if there are any candles around here."

Candles? Such refinements were foreign to him. Silently, he watched as she rummaged around in cabinets until she came up with a couple of half-burned candle stubs. She dug around until she found a pack of unpopped popcorn and poured it into glasses, into which she stuck the stubs.

"*Voilà!*" she said. "We have candles."

He sat down at the table while she lit them. She looked beautiful in the candlelight, and when she took her place across from him, he could almost believe that they were dining in a fine restaurant in some big city, not in a small kitchen in an apartment attached to the Rancho Encantado stable.

She lit into the chili with gusto. "Mmm, this is good," she said.

He'd been a little bit worried that Brooke, because of her nausea, might not be able to eat something as spicy as Mattie's chili. He was pleased to see that this didn't seem to be a problem.

"Who made this?" she asked.

"I told you, a friend."

She raised her eyebrows. "I didn't mean to be nosy."

"Not a girlfriend."

She stared at him. "I didn't imply that," she said coolly.

"You didn't have to. I knew what you were getting at." He went on spooning chili into his mouth, impervious to her raised eyebrows.

"You thought I was fishing for information."

"Sure did."

"Why would I do that when I can eat in the communal dining hall and find out all sorts of things that I really don't need to know about you?"

This only confirmed his suspicion that people discussed him in places that they shouldn't have. "Like what?"

Her cheeks flushed, and she looked away. "You probably know very well what."

"Maybe I don't. Unless it has to do with visiting a certain yellow-painted building hereabouts."

"Bingo," she said. He thought she might be struggling to maintain a disinterested position.

"For your information, I have never been inside that place."

"It is of no matter to me if that's how you wish to spend your time. The only thing is, maybe you'd better think twice before you stint on your duties around the ranch to hang out at Miss Kitti-Kat's."

"I told you, that's not where I go."

"Care to enlighten me?" She shot him an arch look and reached for the butter.

This stopped him abruptly. Only a week or so ago, he wouldn't have wanted to tell anyone about his ongoing work at Jornada Ranch. Suddenly and again, he was on the verge of telling Brooke.

Not a good idea. He stood up and went to the sink, where he refilled his water glass.

"Well?"

When he turned, she was watching him.

He sat down and leaned across the table. "Maybe I'd better tell you a story," he said.

"Go ahead."

He thought for a moment about whether he really wanted to do this. He wouldn't have to tell Brooke everything. He still needed to protect himself and his position with Justine.

"Once there was a boy," he said slowly. "A little boy who lived in a small mining town in Nevada. The family wasn't too respected in those parts. The father drank a lot, and the mother—well, the boy never knew her. Since his father used to beat him with great regularity, he hoped that his mother would show up someday and rescue him."

Brooke had gone still and quiet, and she had stopped eating. He studied her reaction for a moment before plunging ahead.

"The boy didn't do well in school. He couldn't. He didn't get to go every day because someone had to take care of his father, and it was usually him. When a teacher reported his truancy, the state stepped in and sent him to a series of foster homes, where he suffered even more abuse."

Brooke looked stunned and shocked.

"I won't finish the story if you don't want to hear it," he said carefully, keeping his tone level.

She drew a deep breath. "I do want to hear it. Continue, please."

"You're sure?"

"Yes."

"As the boy got older, he rebelled. He ran away from a couple of foster homes and punched a social worker in the eye. He was sent to juvenile detention, where he picked fights with everyone he could. He quit school and hooked up with the rodeo circuit. He stole things that he couldn't afford to buy, and he got into trouble with the law. He spent some time in jail, and no one ever came to see him on visitors' day. His father died in a drunken brawl that he started, which reaffirmed the local people's opinion that the family was no damn good. The boy was now a man, but he was an unhappy man, a man with no purpose in life.''

"Cord," Brooke said. "You were that boy, weren't you?"

He held her gaze and nodded slowly. "Yes, I was," he said.

"Tell me the rest of it."

"When I figured out that my life would never get better until I changed my ways, I decided to walk the straight and narrow. I did well on the rodeo circuit and was starting to be well known. Then I had the accident."

"A rodeo accident?"

"No, ironically enough. I was driving a pickup hauling a trailer with a couple of horses inside when a tractor-trailer rig ran a stop sign and hit us broadside. The horses were injured and had to be put down. I broke my back, got a gash in my chin. For a while I wished I'd been put down, too. That accident may have been the best thing that ever happened to me."

"You had to quit the rodeo, right?"

He nodded. "No way I could ride in competition after they patched up my vertebrae with a couple of steel rods. I had to find me a real job. I landed here at Rancho Encantado because Justine was desperate for a ranch manager and I could do the work. Been here ever since."

Brooke was silent for a time. "What does this have to do with your frequent absences?"

"I'm getting around to that." He leaned back in his chair. "I want to help boys who have had a rotten life.

Boys like me.'' He felt uncomfortable with portraying himself as a do-gooder.

''How will you help them, Cord?''

''By giving them something worthwhile to do with their lives. I don't want to say too much about it right now.''

''Any special reason?''

''So Justine will keep me on until I decide to go. I need the money I earn here, Brooke. If Justine knew that I plan to quit soon, she'd toss me out on my ear.''

Brooke rolled her eyes. ''Cord, that's only because you're neglecting your work here and she thinks you're goofing off. Set her straight about where you are and what you're doing. Surely she'd understand.''

''I doubt it.''

''She seems like a decent person.''

''Decent, yes, but like everyone else in these parts, she's heard stories about my family. I know my reputation around here. It's not good.''

Brooke appeared on the verge of asking questions, but she must have thought better of it. She finished eating her chili and pushed the bowl to one side. ''Cord, why did you tell me this story?''

''I'm not sure.'' It may have had something to do with the fact that she was the only person who had been able to get close to him in a very long time. Or it may have been because she had told him about her pregnancy and made it clear that no one else knew. He felt secure with her, which surprised him.

''Don't worry, I won't betray your confidence.''

''I hope not. My success depends on my earning as

much as I can here at Rancho Encantado before I give my notice.''

''When will that be?''

''Depends.'' He still needed to make small repairs to the little cottage where Mattie and Jonathan would live once he moved into the big sprawling ranch house.

Brooke got up and began to rinse the dishes in the sink. She glanced over her shoulder. ''Would you like to see the diary I found in the old trunk?''

He didn't think he did, but she looked so all-fired enthusiastic. He followed her into the living room, where she turned on a light and slid a leather-bound book down from a shelf over the desk in the alcove.

She sat on the couch and patted the cushion beside her. He joined her, finding it hard to concentrate when they were sitting with their thighs almost touching. Fragrance wafted from her hair, and he was conscious of her graceful hands as she carefully turned the pages of the old book.

''See, here's the page where Jerusha Taggart, the diary's author, listed all the members of the wagon train. My great-great-great-grandmother's name is right here. Her husband, James, was my great-great-great-grandfather. The names beneath theirs are those of their children.''

Cord began to read the diary entry.

November 15, 1849

Today we walked even farther in the desert than usual. We are still hoping to cross the mountains before it gets too cold in the higher elevations. Our wagon master, Mr. Tyson, showed us the map that was given to him by the Mojave Indians. I must say that the journey seems arduous, but Mr. Tyson says—

Cord couldn't read any more. Agitated, he stood up abruptly. "I really should go. We'll need to start out early tomorrow morning."

She shot him a puzzled look. "It's not very late."

He couldn't tell her that seeing the name Tyson written in that diary was more than he could bear. He'd spent most of his life trying to avoid the name's stigma, and he thought he'd succeeded. He'd gone away, become a rodeo star and was making plans for a new life. He had put the past behind him—until now.

"Sorry," he mumbled. He pivoted on his heel and started through the kitchen.

"Do you want to take anything from the refrigerator with you?"

A beer would taste mighty good. He stopped and opened the refrigerator door. The beer was cold in his hand as he turned and saw Brooke standing there, looking hurt.

Oh, great. He hadn't meant to hurt her feelings. All he'd done was to adopt his customary gruff facade so that he could distance himself from his emotions. Usually, it worked. But not now. This time he felt responsible for hurting another human being, one who was becoming important to him.

Brooke met his gaze, refusing to be the one who looked away first. As she watched, his eyes lost their hard glint and softened considerably. The tense lines around his mouth relaxed, and slowly and deliberately, he set the beer can down on the counter. Her brain barely registered this, however. She found herself leaning toward him and hoping that—

She was hoping that he would kiss her.

She had no business wishing for such a thing. But he was no longer a stranger, and she didn't feel rushed, hustled or taken advantage of in any way. Instead, she felt a slow yearning curling in the pit of her stomach, a sensation she had thought she would never feel again. She closed her eyes for a moment, savoring the feeling and the hope that went along with it. The experience with Leo had convinced her that she should put love and sex behind her, but she had been wrong, wrong, wrong.

"Cord," she said unsteadily.

His head dipped closer; his eyes never left hers. There was something compelling in their golden depths, an urgency that made her breath catch in her throat. Her heart started to hammer. At first she intended to push him away, but her resolve evaporated when his arms went around her and pulled her close.

"Let it happen, Brooke," he said. "Don't fight it."

She rested her cheek against his shirt, weary of resistance. Such close contact went a long way toward dispelling her loneliness, and in that moment, she wanted his arms around her forever. They were strong arms, thick with muscle, and they felt like a barrier between her and the rest of the world.

"I—I'm not fighting anything," she said. "I don't know where this is going, that's all."

His voice rumbled in his throat. "Does it have to

go anywhere, Brooke? Can't two people find comfort together without playing games?''

"Games," she said unsteadily, thinking of Leo. "I don't like games."

His beard grazed her cheek. "Neither do I. But I do like you, Brooke Hollister. I like you very much."

She drank in the warm musky scent of him, redolent of the outdoors, of sagebrush and eucalyptus and sun-baked desert rock. The fragrance was uniquely Cord's, didn't remind her of anyone else.

Slowly, his hand came up and tilted her face toward his. "May I kiss you, Brooke?"

"Usually, men don't ask."

"Usually, people don't get off to such a bad start as we did." The corners of his mouth curved upward.

"Yes, Cord, you may kiss me. Only, make it a long one. I'm not in the mood for any other kind." She gave him a tentative smile and then he laughed.

"Neither," he said, his breath warm against her cheek, "am I."

His lips descended toward hers, and she let her breath out in a sigh. He reared back. "What was that sigh all about?"

"Relief that we're finally doing this," she managed to say, which made him chuckle.

Then he kissed her thoroughly and robustly. Her arms went around him, pulling him closer so that she felt his thickly braided chest muscles through his shirt, so that she felt enveloped by his warmth. His lips were firm, his tongue insistent, and his hands came up to burrow through her hair, cupping the back of her head so that she couldn't escape.

Not that she wanted to. He was a good kisser, the kind of man who could knock a girl off her feet with only one kiss. He knew all the variations and had mastered them well. She was tingling from the top of her head to the tips of her toes, ready for more but still unsure whether she should allow this to proceed.

When he finally released her, she clung to him, all but gasping.

"Well? Want to go for another one?"

"I—I think so," she said.

"I know so," he said gently, but this time he turned her so that her back was to the wall and his body pinioned her there. He slid one hand around her waist and flipped off the harsh kitchen light with the other so that the only illumination came from the light above the range. His face was dark above her, but she could imagine the intensity of his expression as his lips first nuzzled her temple, then rained a string of light kisses down her cheek to her lips. To be kissing him, to be tasting his lips and tongue in so leisurely a fashion, was utter pleasure. He took his time about it, learning the contours of her mouth as she wanted him to learn the contours of her body.

Something stirred in the deep recesses of her brain—a flicker of bewilderment that she wanted this man in that way. She shouldn't be thinking of becoming intimate with Cord McCall. She should be focused on the overwhelming task of accepting her new role as a mother. How could she, though, with his lips and teeth and tongue so insistent? With his hand skimming up the curve of her waist to cup her breast? There was nothing tentative about his touch. It was demanding, and there was a fierceness about his kisses now, a change that had crept past her consciousness while she reveled in almost-forgotten sexual feelings.

She wrested her lips away.

"Cord," she gasped against the roughness of his beard. "I don't know about this."

"You seemed to know what you wanted a minute ago," he said, his voice rasping against the smooth skin of her throat. His lips continued down her neck, dipped into the hollow at the edge of her collar.

"I did. I don't." She melted as his thumb and forefinger found her nipple erect beneath her clothes. He caressed it.

"I didn't mark you for a tease," he said close to her ear. "I'm usually right about that."

"I'm not teasing. I just don't know if this is a good idea."

Slowly, his hand slid away from her breast. His weight eased away, and he wore an inscrutable expression.

"If it's not good for you, Brooke, it sure as hell won't be good for me," he said.

She wrapped her arms around herself, already feeling bereft at the absence of his strong embrace. "I have a lot to deal with right now," she said slowly. "I don't need another love gone wrong."

"Who said anything about love?"

This only strengthened her resolve not to bite off more than she could chew. "Nobody, least of all me," she said.

He cocked his head and studied her for a moment. "Maybe there isn't any such thing as love. I sure haven't seen much of it in my lifetime. Maybe all there is for some people is comfort in the night. And maybe that's enough.''

As misplaced as sympathy might seem at this time, her heart went out to him. At least she had known love in her life, first from her parents, then from Leo. Well, maybe that hadn't been love after all, but she had thought so at the time.

''You seem awfully disillusioned,'' she said, straightening her clothes and putting some distance between her and Cord. She reached over and snapped on the overhead light. He was glaring at her, and she supposed she didn't blame him.

''Perhaps. This is the second time you've backed off. Are you sure you aren't disillusioned, too?''

His bold stare made her feel uncomfortable, and his question stopped her cold. Maybe, after Leo, she would always be wary of men and their motives. To remain innocent forever when you were out there in the world taking your licks like everyone else was impossible.

''I don't know, Cord,'' she said heavily. ''I like being your friend, if that counts for anything.''

He stared at her for a long moment. His voice was surprisingly gentle when he spoke. ''It counts for a lot, Brooke,'' he said. He drew a deep breath, exhaled. The silence hung heavy between them.

''We'll leave tomorrow morning at seven for Cedrella Pass,'' he said finally. Then he turned on his heel and went through the door to his apartment. He didn't close the door behind him, and neither did Brooke.

For the first time it stayed open between their two private spaces.

Brooke settled herself into bed with Jerusha Taggart's diary. She had a hard time concentrating on it, however, and at last she put the diary aside. Afterward, she lay awake long into the night, wondering what her reaction would be if Cord decided to come to her bed in the night.

But he didn't. She knew he wouldn't. She found herself imagining his hard body next to hers just the same.

## Chapter Nine

When she stepped out into the stable the next morning, Cord was dishing feed into the horses' troughs with an old coffee can. He turned and greeted her as soon as he saw her, treating her to a long smoldering glance that made her regret, if only momentarily, calling a halt to the previous night's proceedings.

Brooke decided that it was best to remain straightforward and even a little brisk if they were to be together all day. While Cord went into the tack room, she spent a few moments petting the stable cat. She looked up when he reappeared.

"What's this cat's name?" she asked.

"Mrs. Gray. She's not the most friendly feline I ever saw."

"She likes me, I think." She stood.

"Ready to go?"

"Sure. I want to bring some extra water." She went back inside the apartment, and as she opened the door, the cat darted inside.

"No, you can't stay in here," Brooke told her. She picked the cat up and put her out. Mrs. Gray meowed pitifully, but Brooke remained firm. "You'll have to tough it out in the stable," she told the cat.

Cord was waiting for her in the borrowed Jeep when she came out, carrying the bottles of water and a jacket.

"We need to stop at the kitchen and pick up our lunch," Brooke reminded him.

After they loaded the basket of food into the back of the Jeep, they proceeded around the hill that sheltered the old borax mine and started along the rutted track toward the line of mountains to the west. Scudding cumulus clouds cast shadows across the desert landscape, and before they had gone far, a pair of jet-fighter planes from the nearby air force base roared overhead, sketching straight white contrails across the sky. A hot day was in the offing, Brooke thought, but maybe it would be cooler once they started climbing the mountains.

"How is your work going?" Cord asked her after a time.

She shrugged. "The article about Rancho Encantado is still in its early stages. To tell you the truth, I'm much more taken with the diary and with some of the newspaper clippings from the time."

"Why are you so interested in all that, anyway? What's this special project you're so keen to pursue?" His eyes upon her were curious.

"The Cedrella Pass episode would make a good book," she said. "I'd like to write it."

He seemed taken aback. "What kind of book?"

"I'm thinking along the lines of a nonfiction book that traces the families back to their lives in the East, that tells a little about the individuals and follows them through the ordeal.'' She was slowly homing in on the book's focus, and she sensed that the story would be more powerful if she concentrated on the people rather than the place.

''Isn't the whole sorry episode best forgotten?''

Something about his tone of voice caught her attention—a harshness, a misplaced bitterness. She turned to look at him, but his eyes were focused straight ahead on the road and his posture gave nothing away. Still, she chose her words carefully.

''Cord, consider the play of personalities as the settlers travel west, the dangers of crossing the desert and of hostile Indians, the lure of gold in California. It could be exciting reading. Also, I have a personal interest. My great-great-great-grandmother died at the pass. Family lore is that she starved to death because of the wagon master's poor judgment and lack of planning.''

''I see,'' was all he said, but the words held a bleakness and he became very quiet.

At Padre's Creek, the banks of the stream were flanked with cottonwoods and willows, a contrast to the desert beyond, and nearby stood the crumbling ruins of Padre Luís's house. Cord gunned the Jeep through the creek shallows, and she turned to him quizzically. ''You don't seem enthusiastic about my book idea. Why?''

''In my opinion, that old story is better forgotten.''

''What happened at Cedrella Pass is history, Cord, part of the lore about the California gold rush. There are questions that have never been answered. For instance, wouldn't you like to know how Tyson, the wagon master, came into possession of the map that led them into such a dangerous situation?''

"The Mojave Indians gave it to him. Everyone knows that.''

"He must have trusted them. Something must have gone terribly wrong. Tyson's life was also endangered when they got snowed in at the pass.''

Cord's lips tightened perceptibly. "Tyson was an idiot.''

"So it would seem, but the families that split off from the original wagon train at Santa Fe trusted him enough to go with him.''

"They were even stupider than Tyson, wouldn't you say? Taking women and children across the treacherous desert on a route that had never been traveled? The wagons were too big to get through. The party wasted valuable time cutting down trees so that they could pass. Bad weather came, and they were trapped. They're lucky they didn't end up like the Donner party.'' They were approaching a salt flat. Suddenly, he gunned the Jeep engine so that they fairly flew past it.

Brooke knew the story of the Donner party, trapped by early blizzards in the Sierra Nevada a few years before the Tyson group suffered severely in Cedrella Pass. Forty-two people in the Donner party had died, and rumors of cannibalism had haunted gold seekers who followed, most of whom went to great lengths to avoid traveling across the mountains too late in the fall.

Brooke took a deep drink of water, then offered the

bottle to Cord. He declined, and Brooke faced front again. She tried to imagine the wagon train heading toward these formidable mountains, the fear as the travelers realized that a winter storm was approaching.

She recalled one of Jerusha's most compelling journal entries, which touched on the subject.

December 17, 1849

Today our men captured two Indian men as we approached the trail through the pass. The Indians were frightened, as well they should have been, for Mr. Tyson threatened their lives if they did not lead us to the spring. It turned out that the map was incorrect—the spring was located five miles to the north of where it was marked, and Mr. Tyson felt that the Mojaves who gave him the map had deceived him greatly.

We were desperate for water, and the children were crying most piteously from thirst as we made our way to the spring. Though winter is fast closing in, we had no choice but to detour. When we got there, we found an abandoned Indian village occupied by only one old woman. She and the Mojave braves spoke rapidly and angrily, and we could not understand what they said. They allowed us to drink from the spring and water our oxen, as well as replenish our water supply to take with us on the trail through the pass. As we left, however, the old Indian woman screamed curses, which did make Mr. Tyson look very worried.

Since he understands the Mojave tongue, I

asked him what she said. He told me that the old woman had cursed us and our oxen and our wagon train most vituperatively. I asked him if he was afraid, and he did not answer.

Mr. Privette told Annabel and me privately that he believed the Mojave braves were very angry because we'd captured them. It is his belief that we should have treated them in a friendly manner and not held them hostage as we did until they showed us the spring.

Perhaps we are lucky to have escaped this incident with our lives. I continue to worry about Nathan, who is querulous in the manner of sick children. Teensy does not speak much but clings to her beloved china doll, Eliza, her eyes wide and fearful. It takes all her energy to get through the day.

As for the babe in my womb, I felt him move today for the first time. I console myself about the present privations by anticipating our lives in California once we have found gold. It will be a better life for all of us, including this unborn babe.

I mentioned this to poor Annabel in the hope of encouraging her. She did not reply. Annabel was the weakest adult of our party at the outset, and I am concerned about her cough. She has made me promise to look after her children if she does not live to see the goldfields.

Annabel, sick? Annabel, coughing? To Brooke, trying to read between the lines, it sounded as though

Annabel suffered from what was in those days called consumption—tuberculosis.

Brooke had grown to like Jerusha Taggart after reading her diary entries. Clearly Jerusha was a conscientious young mother and was seeking to improve the family's lot by making the trek to California. Brooke already knew that Annabel Privette had died along the way, said to be the victim of Willis Tyson. Had the Taggarts made it to the goldfields? Brooke wasn't sure.

After Cord pointed out a white arrow painted on a boulder, which was the only indication that they had reached the Tyson Trail, the unpaved road became a track, hard going in some places. Cord drove competently and a bit faster than Brooke thought necessary, explaining the area's geology as they went.

The mountains, Cord told her, were a rocky stack of old lava flows. "There's an underground river below us whose source is in the mountains, and the river feeds the seven springs that irrigate Rancho Encantado's valley," he said.

The trail ascended sharply above a wash. Here the mountain slopes were sparsely populated by cholla and cactus, an inhospitable landscape. Farther on Joshua trees in a grove greeted them, their arms crowned with spring blossoms that resembled nothing so much as popcorn balls.

As the Jeep climbed higher, Brooke became fascinated by the change in vegetation. When they reached the summit of the first peak, they entered a forest of junipers. Cord stopped the vehicle. "Here's where we eat lunch," he said.

Brooke climbed down from her seat and took in the view. Ahead, where Brooke imagined that the Tyson party might have expected to see an end to their journey, there were only more mountains, each one seemingly more bleak and barren than the last.

They found shade amid the junipers, where Cord spread a blanket on the ground and Brooke set out the food. There was cold tarragon chicken, a salad, a loaf of crusty fresh bread and a thermos filled with apple cider. The chef had also included several pieces of fruit. It was more than they could eat, and Cord teased her about ordering for four people instead of two.

"Not four people. Three. I'm eating for two," Brooke said, and he smiled.

"Sounds as if you're getting used to the idea of having the baby."

"I am. I'm making plans, deciding where I'm going to live, things like that."

He looked surprised. "You're moving out of L.A.?"

"Not necessarily, but I'll need a bigger apartment. I want the baby to have her own room."

"How do you know it's a girl? It's a little early for an amnio, isn't it?"

"Yes, I think so. I didn't expect you'd know about amniocentesis."

He grinned. "Must have read something about it in one of those dog-eared *Fling* magazines I saw in doctors' offices."

"I'm the one who should have been reading those articles," she said.

"You never did say how you know your baby is a girl."

She leaned back against a boulder. "I just know, that's all." It was because of one of those strange messages that she'd received since she had been here, the kind delivered directly into her ear by a Spanish-accented voice. But she didn't feel like explaining this to Cord, so she changed the subject. "Why haven't you ever married, Cord?" she asked.

He flicked a bread crumb off the blanket and gazed into the distance for a moment. "It wasn't in the cards I was dealt," he said finally.

"You'd be a wonderful father."

"I'm not worthy of children," he said tightly. Then, ignoring her perplexed expression, he began to toss picnic items back into the basket. "Come on, it's time to leave."

As she helped him clean up the site, she pondered what Cord had said. Not worthy of having children? It was a strange thing to say, and it was sad, too, considering how they seemed to love him.

As soon as they had settled inside the Jeep, she spread the map across her lap and studied it as they descended into the valley. On their climb up the next mountain, they found themselves travelling on a series of switchbacks. When they reached the peak, Cord stopped so she could take in the panorama before them.

"I can only imagine how daunting the journey must have been for members of a wagon train who were hoping to reach the goldfields before cold weather set in,'' she said musingly. ''Or two wagon trains, come to think of it.''

''Two? Only one wagon train came through here in 1849. The Tyson party.''

She shook her head, glad that he was showing interest in the facts her research had produced. ''At first, when the six families left Santa Fe, there was one wagon train. But according to Jerusha's diary, three of the families and four single men became distrustful of Tyson and began to fall back so that they wouldn't have to do what he said.''

''You're really into this, aren't you?'' Despite Cord's obvious effort to remain uninvolved, she detected a hint of admiration.

''Sure, why wouldn't I be?''

Cord didn't speak. She sensed that he disapproved of her book project, and in a way, she didn't care. In another way, she cared very much, mostly because she wanted his approval. She wasn't quite sure why, other than she had grown to respect him. Maybe it was that she wanted him to respect her, as well.

''Anyway,'' she went on, ''the party split up before they got to the mountains. Both groups managed to find shelter, but in different places.''

''Are you sure? I never heard the story told that way.'' Cord kept his eyes on the track.

''Why would Jerusha tell it other than it was? Her family, the Taggarts, and my ancestors, the Privettes, and another family named Cokeley stuck together with Mr. Tyson, along with a few single men. The others, who came to be known as the Hennessy group, shunned the Tyson party.''

"You'd think there'd be safety in numbers, that they'd stay together no matter what."

"Eugene Hennessy, the leader of the Hennessy group, hated Tyson with a passion. After a couple of instances when the Mojave map proved wrong, he wanted to cross the desert in the north instead of taking this southerly route. Tyson refused, and it was too late for the Hennessy group to head north on their own."

"Too late because of the snow?'

Brooke nodded. "Winter weather was the main thing they were trying to avoid. Anyway, both groups found shelter in caves in these mountains. The Hennessy group, straggling along separately, ended up several miles from the Tyson party."

"I wonder why I haven't heard about this before."

"No doubt because all the published reports were one-sided. Rescuers reached both groups on the same day. Reporters interviewed members of the Hennessy group, assuming that they spoke for both contingents. Of course, they had negative things to say about Tyson."

"You learned this from Jerusha's diary?"

"There's certainly no mention of it in the history books. Jerusha went into a lot of detail about the Tyson-Hennessy split."

Cord seemed thoughtful as they descended into a canyon where the trail became narrower, in some places barely wide enough for the Jeep to pass. At one point, Cord pointed to the cliffs ahead. "See the cave openings up there?" he said. "That's where we're going." He cast an eye skyward and shook his head. "I sure don't like the look of that," he told her.

Brooke followed his line of sight and saw dark thunderclouds piling up in the west. "Thunderstorm?"

He nodded. "The spring storms in these mountains can be fierce. Let's hope it's traveling north," he said. He appeared to dismiss the possibility of the storm's affecting them, but later, when he thought she wasn't looking, she caught him sending worried glances in that direction.

They rounded a cluster of boulders. "The place we're looking for is right around the next bend. Don't ask me if it was the Tyson party or the Hennessy group who stayed there. Those caves don't come with a guest registry."

She leaned forward in her seat to peer ahead. The sides of the mountain were slabs of sheer rock, and there was little vegetation. "This site doesn't look like a likely place to shelter from anything," she said.

"If they'd had to camp in the open, maybe they all would have died. It gets right cold up here in the winter when the snows come. This trail becomes impassable," Cord replied, and for the first time, she sensed some sympathy for the plight of the travelers.

A sharp incline, a sort of ramp, led downward from the flat promontory. Here, Cord parked the Jeep. "We're going down there," he said, pointing.

She paused, her hand on the door handle. "Is it far?"

"Not very." He exited the Jeep, went around to the back and tucked some items from the picnic basket into the many pockets of his vest. Brooke took her water bottle and strapped it to her belt.

''Be careful not to slip,'' Cord cautioned as they started down the rocky ramp, and he held her arm tightly as they walked. Brooke was thankful for her sturdy hiking boots, which kept her from slipping on the loose rock. She was also thankful for Cord's steady grip.

At the bottom of the incline, she saw a cave opening. It was little more than a fissure in the rock.

''This is it?'' she asked.

Cord nodded. ''I brought a flashlight. We'll go inside.''

They had to enter sideways in order to squeeze through the opening. The cave was tall but not roomy. Cord's flashlight beam revealed a rock-strewn floor and bats nesting above.

''There's not much in the way of creature comforts,'' Brooke said. She kept a wary eye on the bats, which didn't seem to notice their presence.

''There's a bigger cave farther along,'' Cord said.

They stepped outside. The dark clouds had moved closer, and an ominous growl of thunder reverberated from the far mountain peaks.

Cord grimaced. ''Great. A major storm is all we need.''

''I didn't think it rained much in the desert.''

''Any area that receives fewer than ten inches a year of precipitation and has a high evaporation rate qualifies as a desert. The desert down below—'' he jerked a finger back toward where they had come from ''—gets about two inches each year. But we're not in the valley now. We're in the mountains. There's something called the rain-shadow effect.''

"Oh? What's that?''

"The storms that sweep in off the Pacific Ocean are loaded with moisture, but these mountains catch much of it before it reaches the desert. Some of the water lands on coastal communities, but a lot of it remains in the clouds, like those up there. When the clouds reach the mountains, there's nowhere to go but up. The clouds rise—the air cools. Since cold air can't hold as much water as warm air, the water in the clouds condenses and falls as rain or snow. Bad luck for the Tyson and Hennessy contingents back in 1849, and bad luck for us today.''

"At least it's not snow,'' Brooke said glumly as she eyed the gray curtains of rain sweeping sideways in the distance. "Say, Cord, do you think maybe we could make it back to the ranch before the storm hits?''

"Fat chance. We don't want to get caught in a flash flood in one of the narrow canyons. The storm could still pass over, so let's check out the other cave,'' he said.

Brooke tried to ignore the lightning in the distance. "All right, we'll take a look.''

As she followed Cord along the path toward the second cave, she felt a rush of cold air. The wind was picking up, driving dry bits of grass and leaves up against the face of the mountain.

The second cave, redolent with the scent of long-ago campfires, was much larger than the first. Cord beamed the flashlight into the cave's dark recesses.

"Do you mind if I take a look around the back of the cave?" she asked.

"I'll go with you," he said, but he handed her the flashlight so she could direct its beam wherever she wished.

The first thing she found was what appeared to be a horseshoe.

"Mule shoe," said Cord. Brooke tossed it to one side and continued her search, which turned up a buffalo nickel and a large button that might be made of bone. Further exploration along the back wall revealed the standard graffiti: Kilroy wuz here, and Lisa + Greg, 1972.

"I can see that this place is far off the beaten track, but not far enough to keep people away," she said. She saw a narrow opening. "That might be another room," she said.

The room was small, and so dark that at first she thought that the graffiti artists had spared this part of the cave. Then her flashlight beam picked out scribbles near the ceiling. The bit of writing had faded but was still legible. "'Hennessy,'" she read softly after moving closer, "'1849.' Cord, come see."

He bent into the cramped space, his body brushing hers. "That's what it says, all right." She felt his breath against her ear, the warmth of his body close by. She couldn't help it; her heart speeded up.

"This must be where the Hennessy group stayed, not the Tyson party," she said.

"Local lore says that the Tyson party stayed here," Cord said. He moved away from her, back into the darkness, and she wondered what would happen if the flashlight went out. Would she move toward him and he toward her? Would they reach out to each other in the dark? She swallowed, her mouth suddenly dry.

"We'd better check on the storm," he said, his voice echoing off the cave walls, and silently, she handed him the flashlight. He reached back and took her hand, and she followed him to the cave's mouth.

She didn't need to step outside to know that it had already started to rain. A cold rush of air hissed through the narrow opening, and they heard the rain being whipped against the face of the mountain by a rising wind.

"No way we want to go out there," Cord said firmly. "We'll hang around here for a while and hope it passes quickly."

Brooke, thinking that she might as well be comfortable, spread her neckerchief out on the sandy floor and sat on it. "Well," she said brightly, "I guess I'll have a rare firsthand understanding of what it was like to hole up in a cave during bad weather."

Cord sat down beside her and dug a nectarine out of a pocket. "Want some?"

She nodded, and he cut the fruit in half. "We're likely to be here for some time," he said.

They ate the nectarine, and after they had finished, Cord stood up and peered at the ceiling. "Let's build a fire."

Brooke scrambled to her feet. "I'll help carry the wood," she said.

Campers had left a decent supply of firewood, and they toted the wood from its storage space in the shadows. Afterward, Cord gathered leaves and small branches that had blown inside and used them for tinder and kindling. As they worked to start the fire, Brooke had to pull her eyes away from his taut biceps, clearly outlined under his shirt. But there wasn't anyplace else to look in that dim cave, and she found herself studying him in spite of herself. Despite the stiffness that she had noticed when she'd first met him, he moved swiftly, almost gracefully, getting a fire going in no time.

He sat down beside her. "Is that better?"

"Much." The fire, warm on her face, lent an intriguing glow to Cord's features. By firelight, the deep scar on his chin became a jagged, dark shadow, and suddenly, Brooke wanted nothing so much as to trace it with her fingertip. She wondered if it ached during thunderstorms, or if his back hurt from his injury. These questions seemed too personal to ask.

The wind was shrieking and howling by this time, and another cacophony of sound arose, one that Brooke didn't immediately identify.

"Hail," Cord said in response to her questioning look. He went to the cave opening and came back carrying a huge hailstone in the palm of his hand. "Good thing we found shelter," he said. "I wouldn't want to be hit by a couple of these."

Brooke passed him the water bottle and he drank, then handed the bottle back to her when he was finished. "How are you feeling?"

"Fine."

"No queasiness? Sometimes people get nauseated when they travel in the mountains."

"None today. It comes and goes."

They sat in silence, watching the crackling fire and the dancing shadows that it cast on the walls. Once the fire began to warm the space, Brooke took off her jacket and rolled it up so that she could lie on it. The warmth of the fire had a soothing effect, lulling her into a welcome state of relaxation. "Cord," she said after a time, "do you mind talking about your plans for the future?"

He picked up a stray twig, dropped earlier from the bundle of kindling, and traced a line in the dirt on the cave floor. "Depends on what you want to know, I guess."

"How long until you leave Rancho Encantado?"

"Sooner rather than later. I'm not supposed to know it, but the new guy, Pearsall, who came on board a couple of weeks ago, is being groomed to be ranch manager. He'll do a good job."

"That makes you feel free to go," Brooke said.

"Sure it does. Justine has been good to me. She gave me a job when I needed one, and despite our differences, I wouldn't want to leave her in the lurch."

"Will you be moving far from here?"

He took off his vest and spread it on the ground before he lay back, propping himself up on his elbows. "No, I'll be able to frequent the same old hangouts." He shot her a playful look. "And I told you, it's not what everyone seems to think."

"I believe you."

She was startled when he half turned to her and covered her hand with his. "Why would I be interested in anyone at Miss Kitti-Kat's when I see you every day?"

She almost withdrew her hand, then thought better of it. She liked being close to him—perhaps more accurately, close to the possibilities of him. He was a virile, handsome man, and she was a woman susceptible to his charms. Or her hormones were susceptible; she wasn't sure which. Whatever it was, he had a powerful effect on her whenever he was near.

"Cord, maybe we should talk about this."

He turned her hand over and traced one of the lines on its palm. "Go ahead and talk," he said.

"I wasn't thinking of a monologue. What I have in mind is two-way conversation."

He grinned at her. "Isn't that what we've been having?"

"You know what I mean."

"All right, you go first. If I like the topic, I'll join in."

He was teasing her, and this time she did pull her hand away. "You're making light of something that should be treated seriously."

"I didn't mean to."

"Of course you did." She paused. "I don't know why you're interested in a pregnant woman."

"I'm interested in a woman. You. The fact that you're pregnant is incidental."

"You said something last time—"

"Last time what?" He recaptured her hand again, distracting her so that her thought processes became hopelessly jumbled.

"Last time we kissed."

"The only time we kissed, if I remember correctly.

You called a halt to the proceedings, much to my disappointment.''

''I didn't feel right about it. I'm going to have another man's child, and if I understand correctly, you want to make love to me.''

''You've got that right.''

''Of course, just to confuse the issue, last time you tossed in a sentence or two about all there is for some people is comfort in the night, and maybe that's enough. I'm not sure what to make of it. Of you.''

''You think too much, Brooke.''

''I translate what you said to mean that you're not into relationships. I think what you're saying is that you don't believe in love. Well, I do. Or I did.'' She fell silent, troubled by her thoughts.

Cord became serious. ''What I meant to say was that there's been precious little love in my life. As for relationships, it's not possible for me to enter into one with someone who isn't special to me. I don't like revolving doors.''

''Even after what happened to me, I still believe in love,'' she said softly.

''Lucky you,'' he said. There was no irony in his tone, no ruefulness and no sarcasm. Perhaps a bit of envy, but even that was muted.

She settled against him with a sigh, her eyelids drifting closed as she was calmed by the steady drumming of rain outside the cave. Thunder boomed, the wind wailed and lightning rent the air, but they remained snug and comfortable in the cave. As Cord's arm went around her to hold her close, Brooke wished she could feel like this all the time—safe, warm and protected.

## Chapter Ten

Brooke must have dozed off, because a particularly loud clap of thunder startled her so that her eyes flew open.

"Are you resting comfortably?"

To hear Cord's voice so near her ear was surprising, and then she remembered the circumstances. She started to sit up, but he pressed her back. "No reason to move. We're not going anywhere yet." His breath ruffled the hair at her temple.

"How long did I sleep?" she murmured.

"An hour. Maybe less."

"Did you sleep, too?"

"No." He didn't add that he couldn't have slept if he'd tried, considering that his senses were full of her as he cradled her close to his chest. While she slept, he had gazed at her unashamedly, drinking in the dusky shadows her eyelashes cast against her cheeks, wishing that he could slide his free hand up and through her pale hair. She had slept with her lips slightly parted, he could see the tips of her teeth, and once she had sighed and shifted her weight so that it would have been easy to brush his lips against her cheek. He hadn't, but he'd been tempted.

"Cord," she murmured, her voice so low that he had to bend closer to hear.

"What?" The word was more abrupt than he'd intended.

"We could be here a long time."

"Maybe."

"Will they send someone out to look for us?"

"I'm not sure." It seemed doubtful, since he was famous around the ranch for his erratic behavior and frequent absences.

"No one will miss me," she said.

He thought she sounded fearful, so he slid a finger under her chin and tipped her face toward the light cast by the fire. "Don't worry. I'll take care of you."

Her eyes searched his. "I believe you," she said. She was more beautiful than ever in the glow from the fire; her eyes were so wide and trusting. For the first time he was aware of the damp chill in the air.

"Are you warm enough, Brooke?"

She nodded, her eyes never leaving his. He took in the delectable curve of her lips, the smudge of soot on her cheek. He brushed it away, and her hand captured his and held it for a moment against the curve of her jaw. He felt her swallow.

"Oh, Brooke," he said, knowing he was lost. Then his lips were upon hers, capturing them in a kiss more remarkable for its hunger than for its tenderness. He felt her gasp and then she was returning his kiss. He eased her back against the ground so that his weight was full upon her.

"Do you want me to stop?" he demanded.

Slowly, she shook her head. And then her hands were inside his shirt, cool against his skin. He slid one leg between hers, cupped his hands around her breasts. They were warm and full, cresting over the top of her bra.

"Wait," she said, pushing herself up on one elbow while she unfastened hooks and buttons. Clothing fell away to reveal creamy flesh, and then he was out of his shirt and jeans so that he and Brooke were pressed length to length in front of the warm fire.

He ran his hands along the curve of her waist, slid them around her buttocks and inhaled the sweet womanly scent of her skin. His hands moved around to her softly rounded abdomen and lingered there. He thought guiltily of the child she carried; was it okay to be doing this?

She must have sensed his hesitation. "It's all right," she whispered, the words tickling his ear. She slid her hands over his and moved them lower.

He closed his eyes, thinking that he had never known a woman who was more willing. He found what he sought and let his fingers circle gently, rewarded when she sighed and shifted closer.

Her hands upon him were gentle but firm; she understood how to touch a man and to elicit the most thrilling sensations. This was more than he had expected, and he groaned with pleasure.

She drew him into a long and intense kiss, a marvel of lips and teeth and tongue that left him gasping. "Woman, what are you trying to do to me?" he said.

Her face was gilded by the firelight, her eyes deep blue pools.

She laughed lightly, her lips curving against his cheek. "I want to make love to you so that you'll remember me when I'm gone," she said, and he thought at first that she was joking. There was no time to mull this over, however, because she drew his head down to her breasts so that he could kiss one, then the other. The nipples were large and brown, the color of maple syrup and nearly as sweet, but they tasted of Brooke, the essence of her. Her back arched until it was all he could do to hold back. He didn't want this to be quick; he wanted to experience each and every sensation to the max. But she was not in a mood to wait.

"Cord," she said, her voice a plea, and she wrapped her legs around him and urged him closer, until he felt himself slipping into her warm wetness, sliding into that dark place between her legs, so mysterious and so unknown to him until now.

Now there was nothing about her that was unfamiliar to him; now he knew her body as well as he knew his own; now she was a part of him. And there was nothing dark, nothing mysterious about any of this. All was revealed to him in those moments of first union, all that he had ever wanted to know about the universe and everything in it. Because she was everything, this Brooke, this woman, this sweetness, this pleasure, this—ah, yes, this light that burst behind his eyelids with all the passion and pent-up longing that he'd held back since the first moment he'd seen her.

She was with him all the way, her breath a fierce

urging in his ear, then on his lips, then whirling him along into a wild ride that swept him into regions of the heart he had never known existed. Her name was on his lips at the height of their passion, and his name escaped from hers, the words blending as their bodies convulsed as one.

In the breathless moment when he collapsed against her, spent, he still felt at one with her. He did not feel the immediate loneliness that had always overtaken him after making love. He felt connected, resurrected, at peace.

They spiraled together down off that incredible high, capable only of sighs and whispers.

"Brooke?"

"Mmm."

"Are you all right?"

"Yes." The word was a sibilant syllable against his throat. Her hand curved trustingly amid the hair on his chest. When he looked down at her, he saw that her eyes were luminous, and he wanted to sink into that calm blueness and be lost forever. "Make me believe in love, too, Brooke," he whispered. For an answer, she lifted his hand to her lips and kissed the palm.

He cradled her close, aware of every curve, every bit of flesh that pressed so tightly against his. And then they slept, plunged into a deep and dreamless sleep that enclosed them in each other's world, where he wanted to be for the rest of his life.

She had said that she wanted to make love to him in a way that he would remember after she had gone. His last thought before sleep was that she had made love to him in a way that made him sure that he never wanted her to go. He never wanted to be without her. Never, as long as he lived.

WHEN THEY AWOKE it was morning and the storm had ended. Self-consciously they dressed, pretending not to look at each other, and emerged from the cave into a world washed fresh and new by the rain.

"I'll stroll up to the Jeep and see what food's left in the picnic basket. I think there's bread and more fruit," Cord said. He dropped a light kiss on her cheek before he headed up the path.

Brooke found a pool of water collected in a hollow of a rock and used it to wash her face. There was no mirror, but she thought she must look different this morning. After making love with Cord, she certainly felt different. She felt washed as clean and new as the world this morning, ready to start life afresh.

Cord brought bread, salad and the thermos of cider. They toasted the bread on sticks over the remains of the fire, ate and then carefully quenched the fire.

"There's one fire that can't be put out," Cord said. Then he pulled Brooke to him and kissed her thoroughly, recapturing briefly the passion of the previous night. She clung to him, unsure what he expected now. Last night he had asked her to help him believe in love, too, but her request could have fueled the intensity of the moment. She'd always believed that a real relationship took time to develop, and the one thing they didn't have was time. She would leave Rancho Encantado to return to L.A. soon, and he was moving somewhere else. For a moment a scene flashed before her: running into Cord somewhere, sometime. She would introduce him to her baby daughter, and he would make a napkin mouse to amuse her. It wouldn't happen, couldn't happen.

''We'd better get back,'' she said.

He kept his arm around her shoulders. ''If you like, we could go over the next ridge and take a look at the caves there,'' he said. ''If what Jerusha wrote is correct, they could be the real location of the Tyson party's shelter.''

''Don't you need to get back to work?''

His laugh was tinged with irony. ''Justine told me to show you around, didn't she?''

Brooke didn't want to be parted from him. She wanted to be with him as much as possible. In the difficult days that were to follow, she would have these moments with Cord to remember, to cherish, to sustain her through bearing a child and raising it alone.

She smiled at him. ''Okay,'' she said, and he took her hand as they headed up the slope back to the Jeep.

She gave up trying to figure out what was going on between them. Maybe, as Cord had said, comfort in the night was enough.

CORD FELT GOOD riding beside Brooke up the mountain, knowing that his absence was, for once, sanctioned by his employer and that Pearsall, his heir apparent, was capable of managing crises. He didn't even try to stop himself from glancing over at Brooke now and then and marveling at what had passed between them last night. He hadn't dreamed that she could be so passionate, so spirited a lover.

He reached over and placed a hand on her knee.

"It was good, you know," he said.

"Last night?"

"What else?"

She smiled, and he saw a momentary shimmer of sadness in her eyes. "Comfort in the night?" she said, and he understood what she meant.

"More than that," he said quietly.

He thought she wanted to say something, and he knew what it would be. She wanted to ask, "How much more than comfort?" But she didn't and he knew why. Self-preservation demanded that she not put her emotions out there to be trampled on. He was sure that she didn't have a clue about his deepening feelings for her, and he knew he'd better make them clear before long.

But now they were drawing near to the second group of caves. "See up there?" he said, removing his hand from Brooke's knee and pointing toward the shadowed openings in the cliff ahead.

"How could anyone get up that high?"

"There's a path."

"How far away are we?"

"A few miles, but this location would have been pretty remote before the railroad blasted out some of the rock."

"I didn't know a train ever came through here."

"The railroad was going to build tracks so they could haul borax to the coast, but they abandoned the project when the old mine near Rancho Encantado closed."

He pulled the Jeep into the shade of the cliff and turned off the ignition. "From here we hike," he said.

Their walk took the better part of an hour, and when at last they stood before the cave openings, Brooke said, "Are you sure we can get up there?" She studied the openings in the wall above them.

"Yes, and with minimal danger to life and limb. Are you feeling okay?"

"Still no morning sickness," she said. "Maybe all this fresh air agrees with me."

Cord led the way as they climbed to a narrow road that was little more than a ledge. He was glad that Brooke was so surefooted and confident as they began to ascend, but he held tightly to her hand as they made their way along.

When finally they stopped outside the first cave, Brooke turned and looked back. "Whew," she said. "I'm glad I didn't look before we made it to the top." They could see the Jeep where they had left it, from this distance as tiny as a toy.

Cord had already sized up the entrances to the caves. He heaved and pushed aside a pile of rocks so they could enter the nearest one. Once inside, they realized that this was a large cave, but they saw nothing of interest but a couple of broken dishes.

"These don't look so old," Brooke said after picking up some of the shards and inspecting them.

"Campers," said Cord. "Maybe vagrants."

The next cave was a little harder to enter because the opening was in the roof. This meant that they had to lower themselves inside, which wasn't difficult due to a flat projection of rock below the opening. Cord went first, then turned to help Brooke as she skinned through the narrow aperture.

This cave was larger than the last one and had a rock platform bordering the back wall. The remains of what appeared to be an old ladder lay at its base.

Brooke peered up into the gloom, where Cord's flashlight picked out drawings on the rock.

"Indian petroglyphs," Cord told her dismissively.

Brooke disagreed. "I could believe that if one of them didn't resemble a prairie schooner." She moved in for a closer view, but then her eye was caught by a faint scrawl at eye level on the rock wall directly in front of her.

"Look, Cord! Words!"

He trained the flashlight beam on the rock and saw that these weren't only words; they were names. He could barely make them out. James Privette. Annabel Privette. Melissa Privette. Jody Privette. Lucy Privette. Frank Taggart, Jerusha Taggart, Nathan and Teensy Taggart. Then came the names of another family, the Cokeleys, followed by those of Willis Tyson and three single men, Jarvis Wagner, Melvin Stone and someone referred to only as Albrecht. "We live here," it said.

"'We live here.' If I needed proof, here it is." Brooke's eyes were glowing with the thrill of discovery.

Cord did not feel Brooke's exhilaration; instead, he felt an aversion to reading the names, especially that of Willis Tyson.

"Brooke, let's go."

"Go? Go now? Don't you see what this discovery means to me, Cord? My great-great-great-grandmother lived in this cave and probably died here. To me this is hallowed ground." She stared at him for a moment, but he was unable to summon even the slightest enthusiasm for this place. It made him feel uncomfortable.

Her eyes beseeched him. "Cord, now that I'm here, I want to see all of the cave. I grew up hearing about Annabel Privette. Reading Jerusha's diary has made me realize how the women Forty-niners had dreams of making life better for their children. Annabel and other women like her died in the attempt to attain those dreams, and few people know or care about their sacrifice. I realize now what the slant of my book should be. I want to write about the women of Cedrella Pass."

Cord thought that the world could do without one more line of print on what had happened here. But there was no holding Brooke back.

"I'm going up there," she said, pointing to the platform.

"Not so fast. The ladder may not be safe."

She jiggled it experimentally. "I think it will bear my weight. Will you hold it for me?"

Cord let out a long breath. To deny her anything when she was in this mood was impossible. "All right, Brooke." He handed her the flashlight. "You go, but you go alone. I'll wait for you here. It wouldn't do for the ladder to break behind us, leaving us both stranded up there with no way down."

The ladder remained stable as Brooke climbed it, but he held his breath when she had to scramble up the last few feet of the rock face because the ladder was so short.

"Is everything all right?" he called up to her.

"Fine. Don't worry."

He stared up at the glow of light overhead, wishing he'd brought two flashlights. Down in the cave's lower level, he was alone in the dark, alone with his thoughts. Alone with his memories of his childhood, a miserable time that he'd rather forget, and alone with the boy he had once been, a boy called Bucky Tyson. He'd been sure that he'd left that boy behind, but now, just when he was getting his life together and hoping to make a difference to boys like the one he had been, Bucky turned up.

Would he ever get over being Bucky Tyson? Would he ever be able to leave that name and all that it meant behind?

At the moment, he didn't think so.

ONCE BROOKE REACHED the platform, she lay quietly for a moment while she regained her breath. Then she stood and focused the beam of the flashlight around the wide chamber.

"Brooke, let's make this quick." Cord's voice drifted up from below. He sounded annoyed.

"I haven't even seen anything yet," she called back. Water dripped somewhere in the shadows, and a musty smell hung oppressively in the air. She located a shallow pool fed by a runnel that seemed to originate in a crack in the cave wall, and tasted the water. It was sweet, not salty. The Tyson party could have drunk it. Would have had to drink it, considering the lack of streams around here, she realized as she swung the flashlight beam slowly around her.

This upper region of the cave was a long and spacious chamber divided by an outcrop of stalactites near a pile of rubble. As she edged around this obstacle, a flash of color amid the gravel and debris caught her eye.

"Brooke? What the hell's going on up there?" Cord yelled, exasperated.

"Please don't get impatient. I've found something." She prodded the bit of color with her boot. It was fabric, faded and worn. She bent to pick it up.

It was the remains of a small doll. The china head was mostly intact, but its hair was gone, and the clothes were little better than rags. The doll was old, the clothes obviously homemade. This was the kind of doll that a child with the Tyson party might have chosen to accompany her on the long journey. Was it Teensy Taggart's beloved doll, Eliza, mentioned in her mother's diary? She padded the doll's head carefully with her neckerchief and tucked it deep in her jacket pocket.

Further exploration revealed nothing more of interest other than a few rusty bits of metal that gave her no clue to their past. She nudged them with the toe of her boot, noticing that the flashlight beam had grown weak.

"I'm coming," she called.

"Thank goodness." Cord's exasperation had turned to downright irritation.

She started to back cautiously down the ladder. "Careful," Cord said. "You may have weakened some of the rungs on the way up." His anxious face peered up at her.

"Don't worry. I'm almost—" And then one of the rungs gave way, crumbling to dust beneath her boot.

With a little cry, she fell into Cord's arms.

"Are you all right?"

She still held the flashlight, and the weakened beam danced crazily around the cave walls. "I'm fine."

"We'd better get back to the ranch. It's past lunchtime."

He'd gone remote and stony, and she didn't know why.

"Is everything okay?" she asked, putting a decent distance between them before brushing the dust from her clothes.

His face remained impassive. "Sure. I need to check on some things at the ranch, that's all."

His change in mood detracted from her elation at what she'd found. As they began the long ride back to Rancho Encantado, she tried to occupy herself with planning how to write the book she had in mind, but she kept wondering why Cord remained so uncommunicative. True, avoiding wind-driven storm debris and clumps of uprooted vegetation made driving difficult at times, but that wouldn't account for his present mood. He had been cooperative and helpful until she'd discovered the names of the Tyson party on the rock wall in the cave. Then she had begun to sense a withdrawal on his part, a pulling away.

"Cord," she ventured when they had reached the salt flats and left the mountains behind. "Is something bothering you?"

He kept his eyes front and clipped his words. "It has nothing to do with you."

She hated it when he wouldn't look at her. "All right, so what is it?"

"I don't want to talk about it." If she read his mood right, something was eating him up inside and she had no idea what it could be. His attitude so unnerved her that she subsided without saying anything more. Perhaps, she consoled herself, he would open up to her in time, but they had little of that left to them.

When they reached the stable, she half turned in her seat and asked him to drop by her place for a late lunch.

"I'd better check in with the guys at the barn," he said.

"How about dinner?" she asked.

She was totally unprepared for what happened next. Cord drew a deep breath and took her hand in his. "Brooke, I need some space. I want to cool things down for a while."

The words hit her with all the shock of being unexpectedly drenched with cold water. She was so stunned that at first she couldn't speak. She felt her face flush, and she couldn't breathe.

"Why?" she managed to ask, feeling like a fool as soon as the word had escaped her lips.

He paused and gazed off into the distance to where men were herding cattle into chutes near the barn.

"It has nothing to do with you," he repeated. "In fact, it has everything to do with me."

Her heart sank, heavy as a stone, and seemed to lodge in her stomach. This had all the earmarks of the speech she had heard before, from Leo. The "You're a very nice person but I'm not ready to commit" speech.

"All right," she said, staring at him as though seeing him for the first time. He was a man, after all, like so many others. He was willing to emote and to listen and to exhibit all the other sterling qualities women wanted, until he got what he wanted. Then it was "So long, goodbye, farewell and I'll see you around."

She managed to insert the proper amount of chill into her tone. "Thanks, Cord, for taking me to the caves. You were an excellent guide."

"Brooke, wait," he said urgently, but she was out of the Jeep and slamming the door before he could say more.

She didn't look back at him. She was sure he would be staring after her with a perplexed frown. They never knew, these guys. They never understood the pain their actions caused the women who had learned to care about them and trust them and yes, even love them.

The message light on her phone was blinking, but she ignored it and went straight into the bedroom, where she thought she'd indulge in a good cry, followed by a hot shower. Nothing like all that steam to clear up a stuffy nose after you've been crying over a man.

But as soon as she entered the bedroom, it became obvious that she couldn't throw herself across her bed and sob out her pain after all. Mrs. Gray, the stable cat, was having kittens there.

# Chapter Eleven

If anything could have diminished the pain of Cord's dismissal, this was it. Brooke had never seen an animal giving birth before, and she was so astonished that she sank to her knees beside the bed to watch the proceedings.

"How did you get in here?" she murmured, but Mrs. Gray only blinked tolerantly before getting back to business. Brooke guessed that the cat had somehow slipped in as someone from Housekeeping had gone in or out.

One kitten had already been born, a tiny coal-black mite. It didn't look like any cat that Brooke had ever seen; its eyes were tightly closed and its ears were no more than tiny flaps positioned way down on the sides of its head.

Mrs. Gray didn't seem to be in serious pain. Instead, she appeared to be concentrating on the task of bringing her kittens into the world. A second kitten was born almost immediately, and Brooke watched quietly as Mrs. Gray bit through the amniotic sac and briskly washed her baby with her tongue. The new arrival was a gray tabby with a white face, and it made little mewling sounds as its mother first checked it over and then directed it toward its littermate.

"Good job," Brooke told her, and she could have sworn that the mother cat smiled briefly before she got back to birthing her third kitten. This one was solid gray and looked almost like its mother. Then, apparently knowing her work was done, the mother cat nosed it toward its siblings and positioned herself so that they could nurse. Finally, she settled back with a contented sigh.

So this was what the miracle of having babies was all about! This singleness of purpose, this loving concern, and yes, pride in one's offspring. When she sensed that Mrs. Gray wouldn't mind, she eased herself up on the bed and stroked the soft gray fur. Mrs. Gray closed her eyes, dozing off for a well-earned nap.

Brooke lay on the bed beside her, one hand cupping her own slightly convex abdomen. When the time came, she hoped she would give birth as efficiently and uncomplainingly as Mrs. Gray.

"We'll be all right, the two of us," she whispered to her baby-to-be. Suddenly, a new knowledge hit her so hard that she had to close her eyes to absorb it: she wanted this baby. And she loved this baby. She didn't have to wait until it arrived to feel affection for it. She loved it now. She loved it for what it was, a new human being. She loved it for its potential, for what it would be, for what this new person would mean to others and what it would mean to her.

Stunned and enlightened by this new knowledge, she got up and wandered through the apartment in a daze. The phone began to ring, and as if in a dream, she picked up the kitchen extension on her way past. She was unprepared for the voice she heard. It was Felice, bringing her back to reality.

"Brooke? Thank goodness you're there! I've been trying to reach you for hours. Why don't you answer your cell phone?"

"Well, I—um, cell phones don't work here because Rancho Encantado is surrounded by mountains." Bringing herself back to the here and now was difficult, and as she did, she remembered yesterday's scene with Cord in all its miserable detail.

"I called about Malcolm Jeffords, Brooke. He's agreed to the interview."

"When?"

"Tomorrow afternoon. I'll need the article by the end of the month, so you'd better head back to L.A. right away. There's no problem, Brooke, I hope."

"This comes as a big surprise. I'm not through with my work here. I'm planning a book on the Cedrella Pass incident, and it could be big."

"That's wonderful, but you can return to Rancho Encantado as soon as you're through with the interview. I'll tell Jeffords's manager you'll be there, okay?"

"Be where?" Clearly there was no arguing with Felice.

"At the Jeffords estate in the Hollywood Hills. You'll have to check in with his security guys—they'll give you a badge at the gate. I know he'll be evasive and difficult, but I want you to be sure to ask Jeffords about those monkeys. Like, does he dress them in little clothes? Are they kept in zoo cages? What's with them, anyway? And of course if you can find out about—''

Brooke blanked out the rest of Felice's ramblings. ''Look, Felice, I'd better call you back. There's a lot going on here right now.''

She barely heard Felice's outraged squawk as she replaced the phone in its cradle.

Now was the time to head for the shower and that cry she'd promised herself. Never mind that she could return to Rancho Encantado to finish research for her book or that she knew exactly the direction that the book should take. She didn't even care that the Malcolm Jeffords piece would give her career a needed boost.

Everything was going right on the professional front, but her personal life was a mess.

CORD WAS BUSY for the rest of the day, overseeing the roundup of cattle into livestock pens, but his mind wasn't on the task. Instead, it was back at Cedrella Pass, remembering the light in Brooke Hollister's eyes as he reached for her. He would never forget the joy of her expression or the warm and sweet way she had nestled against him, with the storm roaring outside and the fire casting a golden glow across her lovely features. It had felt as if the two of them were all alone in the world, with only each other for comfort in the storm.

Though the storm had been a bad one, the danger of being caught in it hadn't fazed Brooke. Somehow, her strength hadn't surprised him. He was willing to bet that Brooke Hollister would be one tough cookie whenever the going got rough. She'd be a hell of a life partner.

A life partner. A partner in life. Someone who would stick by you when things got tough, who would be fierce in love and steadfast under fire. In other words, she'd be an ideal wife.

He didn't need a wife. He didn't know why he was speculating about Brooke's suitability for the job, especially since he was the one who had called a time-out. And he needed space, as he'd said, to mull over the terrible things that a Tyson had done to the people for whom he'd accepted responsibility.

Suddenly, guiltily, Cord wasn't thinking of the light in Brooke's eyes when he had pulled her close or the way they had cuddled all night in the cave. He was recalling how that light had dimmed and gone out when he'd said he needed some space. Now, with the perspective that even such a short time allowed, he couldn't help cursing himself for a fool because he'd been so detached and preoccupied on the ride back from the caves. He should have told her right then why he was acting that way. He should have explained who he was and why seeing the names of Willis Tyson's victims written on the wall of the cave had brought forth such feelings of revulsion and self-hate.

"Hey, boss, you want to close that gate? We're almost finished here."

Cord jerked to attention. "Sure thing, Dusty," he said hastily. Dusty grinned and shook his head as if to rebuke him for not being on the ball.

He'd get it over with tonight. He'd knock on

Brooke's door, come clean with her. He'd tell her what he should have revealed in the first place—the rest of the story.

Unfortunately, it was so late by the time he got back to the stable that he abandoned his plans to see Brooke. The windows of her apartment were shaded and dark, and he figured that she'd been exhausted by the events of yesterday and today. He certainly was.

He went alone to bed and fell into a deep and dreamless sleep. The next morning he woke up and listened for sounds coming through the thin walls from Brooke's apartment. He didn't hear any, so he dressed and went out into the stable to saddle Tabasco.

He was surprised to find Justine waiting for him, striding back and forth and looking impatient.

"I'm glad you're here," she said pointedly.

He pulled his saddle down and led Tabasco out of his stall. Justine fell in right behind him.

"You're being taken off the Brooke Hollister detail, effective immediately," Justine said. "Today I want you to spend some time with Pearsall, the new guy, and tell him about our breeding program."

Keeping his face expressionless, Cord threw a blanket across Tabasco's back and settled the saddle upon it. "Oh? Any reason I'm relieved of my job with Brooke?" He couldn't help wondering if she'd complained about him. Surely he hadn't given her any reason to do that.

"Brooke left this morning. She didn't say when she would be back."

Cord was positive that he hadn't heard Justine correctly. "She what?" His stomach did a dive, turned over.

"Brooke went back to L.A. She said she had to do an important interview. Oh, and Cord, don't forget to mention to Pearsall how I have plans for buying more broodmares. I'll want him to give me some pointers on their selection. Another thing, Mrs. Gray had her kittens last night. I've moved mother and babies to the Big House for a while." Without waiting for a reply, Justine wheeled and walked out of the stable, her mind clearly on other things after dropping this bombshell on his life.

Cord stared after Justine as she headed back toward the Big House. He couldn't believe that Brooke was gone. Worst of all, he couldn't believe how devastated he was at the news.

He shut Tabasco in his stall and rushed back to his apartment, where he slammed open the unlocked door to her kitchen. "Brooke? Brooke!" No answer, everything neat. He flung the refrigerator door open, saw that there was no food.

He went into the living room. Television behind the closed doors of the pie safe, afghan neatly folded on the couch. Computer alcove empty of computer, books and papers. Bed neatly made, no personal items on the nightstand. The bathroom smelled of cleaning spray. Brooke was gone, all right. Good and gone.

He knew he had hurt her feelings yesterday, and he should have thought things through before saying what he did. But he'd had no idea that she would run out on him like this, none at all.

She had left before he could tell her about Bucky Tyson. And she had left before he'd told her he loved her.

AN ENTHUSIASTIC JUSTINE had urged Brooke to take the research materials she'd found at the ranch back to L.A. with her for further study. She'd even promised to stock her book in the gift shop when it was published. Not that Brooke was thinking about the book today. First she had to interview Malcolm Jeffords, then she had to finish her article on Rancho Encantado and after that—well, after that, she'd start work on the book. She'd find a bigger apartment. And she'd get over Cord McCall if it was the last thing she did.

For now, her concern was the important Jeffords interview. She approached his estate in the Hollywood Hills with a certain amount of trepidation. After all, he was reputed to be difficult.

A small stone house blocked the way once she passed through a pair of wrought-iron gates, and uniformed security guards emerged from it to write down her license-tag number and issue her a plastic ID card on a chain.

She left her car in the visitors' parking area and was driven in a golf cart down a long winding road to the Jeffords mansion. The road led through a grove of trees, and when they emerged, she saw the curve of roller-coaster tracks in the distance. That would be Jeffords's famous amusement park.

The mansion was built of honey-gold stone and was impressively large, with gothic windows and a copper roof. Jeffords's publicist hurried out to meet her and conducted her to the poolside terrace. Jeffords, smiling and attentive, came forward to meet her, swim trunks his only apparel and a monkey clinging to his neck.

Brooke, remembering the admonition that Jeffords didn't shake hands because he thought it spread germs, clasped her hands at her waist. She turned down his offer of a chocolate ice-cream soda, saying, "I never drink when I'm working"—a quip that he seemed to find hilarious. Encouraged by this auspicious beginning, she sat down under a table umbrella and turned on her tape recorder, keeping up inconsequent chitchat with Jeffords all the while.

When she flipped open her notebook, Jeffords focused wide blue eyes on her and grinned. "Anything you want to ask, go ahead," he said in his trademark gravelly voice. He unselfconsciously took out a mirror and smoothed an eyebrow, then gave the mirror to the monkey, which chattered excitedly and did the same thing.

Brooke began the interview, easing into the questions that Felice wanted her to ask by talking about Jeffords's childhood and letting him become more comfortable with her.

One thing for sure, she reflected as Jeffords began to regale her with stories about his private zoo: this was a long way from Rancho Encantado. A long, long way. Unfortunately, Rancho Encantado was where she'd left her heart.

CORD WAS BESIDE HIMSELF with regret and worry. He would find her. He had to find her. What if he never saw Brooke again? What if he'd lost her forever?

For the first time in his life he had met a woman whom he'd consider marrying. He didn't know if she'd want him. He wasn't much. But he had to know, damn it. He had to know if she felt the same way about him as he felt about her.

He called Directory Assistance and found a phone number for Brooke Hollister in Los Angeles. He rang the number, but no one answered.

Never mind. He'd call again. Again and again and again if necessary.

AFTER HER INTERVIEW with Malcolm Jeffords, Brooke phoned Felice Aronson, who was on her way home from the *Fling* office, and suggested dinner. They met at their usual place, and Felice pumped Brooke about her interview with the famous rock star.

"He seems like a sad little boy," Brooke said reflectively. "He wants people to like him. The monkeys are his only friends. I'm going to portray him as an innocent, a victim of a lost childhood that he's trying to recapture by having fun at his own amusement park and keeping monkeys as pets."

"So why does he keep so many monkeys?"

"He sees them as little people who are uncritical and sweet." She'd ordered chili, but she pushed it away. It didn't taste nearly as good as the chili that Cord's friend had made.

"Oh, brother," Felice said with a groan.

"Don't worry, it'll be a fantastic article. The interview went well."

Felice smiled at her. "With you to write it, Brooke,

I'm not worried at all. Tell me, how are you doing with the Rancho Encantado piece?''

"Completed the research. All I have to do is finish writing it. I'll do that this week." Would she, though? Even though she didn't want to admit it to Felice, she was stuck. She'd never figured out what to write after the lead that led nowhere.

Felice cocked her head and studied Brooke's face thoughtfully. "You're looking wonderful, Brooke. The makeover must have agreed with you."

"To be honest, Felice, I didn't have the full makeover. I had a massage with aromatherapy and I tried foot reflexology, but I never made it to the hairdresser or the makeup artist."

"You've done *something* to yourself," Felice said, giving her a quick once-over.

"I—oh, Felice. I have something to tell you." There was no avoiding the announcement of her pregnancy any longer, and furthermore, she was eager to tell Felice.

"O-*kay*," Felice said, looking ready to dish.

"I'm pregnant. And I think I'm in love."

"You're joking, right?" Felice knew about Brooke's troubles with Leo. She probably didn't expect her to have found someone else so quickly.

"No joke. I'm serious."

"That was fast work, Brooke. And you already know you're pregnant?"

"The baby is Leo's, and he wants nothing to do with it. I met a man at Rancho Encantado."

"What man?"

"A wonderful one."

"When do I get to meet him?" Felice asked.

"Probably never." Brooke said the words with as little emotion as possible, but she was still shattered over her experience with Cord. Briefly, she explained what had happened, and when she had finished, Felice looked sad and concerned.

"I'm sorry, Brooke."

Brooke's eyes filled with tears. "First Leo, now Cord. What am I doing wrong?"

"Perhaps you pick the wrong guys, that's all."

"Maybe," but she knew that Cord was right for her. He had all the qualities she wanted in a man. And he was unavailable to her for reasons that she didn't understand.

"I'm going to concentrate on having this baby, and I'm also going to write a book," she told Felice. "Those two things should keep me so busy that I won't have time to mourn the loss of Cord McCall." It wouldn't keep her from loving him, however. She would love him forever, hold the memories of their times together close in her heart.

"If you ever want to talk, Brooke, I'm always here for you," Felice said understandingly.

All Brooke could do was smile through her tears. And pay the check, since it was her turn.

ON THE NIGHT that Brooke left, Cord had just hung up after trying to reach her for the umpteenth time, when his phone rang. He clicked it on, hoping that he'd hear Brooke's voice on the other end. But it wasn't Brooke; it was Mattie.

"Cord, I—" She didn't continue the sentence, and she sounded out of breath.

He was instantly on alert. "Mattie, what's wrong?"

"I can't—can't seem to catch my breath. My side hurts. I might be having a heart attack. Can you come over here, Cord? I think I need to go to the hospital, but I can't leave Jonathan."

Cord clapped his hat on his head and retrieved his keys from the dresser. "I'll be there as fast as I can. Call 911. I'll send someone over to look after Jonny and sit with you until they get there."

"Okay, Cord."

"Phone me back after you've called 911, Mattie."

"I will."

They hung up and he dialed the number of the Stewarts, a family who lived about a mile away. Dinah Stewart was a competent mother of three and a registered nurse; her husband, Gil, was a no-nonsense rancher. One or the other of them could be counted on to go to Jornada Ranch and keep things under control until he arrived.

Dinah answered the phone, and he rapidly explained the situation to her.

"Don't worry," she said briskly. "I'll leave right now."

"I'll see you soon," he told her.

Cord rocketed out of the parking area in his pickup at breakneck speed, and he paid no attention to speed limits on the way. When he arrived at Jornada Ranch, he was greeted by flashing red-and-blue lights atop an ambulance. He found Mattie lying on a gurney, the center of a small cluster of emergency workers. She grasped Cord's hand when she saw him. Her grip was weak, but her smile was broad.

"I'm so glad you're here," she said gratefully.

Dinah appeared in the doorway. "I can take Jonathan to my house, put him to bed with my Ryan. You go with Mattie to the hospital, Cord."

So Cord rode with Mattie in the ambulance and held her hand, encouraged her in the emergency room and was beside her all night and part of the next day. Her doctors concluded that she had not had a heart attack but a bout of indigestion. Nevertheless, she was at risk for heart disease, and the false alarm was a warning that she should change her lifestyle.

After he took her home the next day, he sat her down at the kitchen table for a serious talk. "All right, Mattie," Cord told her sternly. "I'm getting your niece Glenna to come in and do housework. She can look after Jonathan and supervise your diet. Is that all right with you?"

"What will I do all day?"

"Place orders, answer the phone and be my right arm just like you are now."

Mattie sighed. "All right, Cord. It makes sense, I guess."

"Sure it does. And Glenna will be fun to have around, you'll see." Glenna was a vivacious mother of two, married and in her thirties. Her kids often played with Jonathan, and they could accompany her when she came to work. Cord knew she was looking for a job where she could keep her children with her, and he'd already planned to bring her on board in some capacity when Jornada Ranch opened for business.

"Glenna is a treasure," Mattie said. "It will be good to have her around more often."

"How would you like to have me around more, too?" Cord asked.

"You, Cord? Are you planning to leave your job at Rancho Encantado?"

"It's time. I'll tell Justine today." He'd make do with the money he'd saved plus his insurance settlement from the accident. He could finish work on the ranch himself and not have to pay others to do it for him.

"Having you here full-time would be wonderful." Mattie zeroed in on him with a look. "Something's different about you," she said. "I noticed it last time you visited."

"Different? What do you mean?"

"Something good. Tell me, Cord, have you met someone new?"

"Aren't you being a little nosy?" He feigned indifference, though he was already familiar with Mattie's intuition, if that was what it was. Being half Shoshone, she claimed to have shamanistic powers of some sort. Her uncle had been a medicine man, and her mother had been a wisewoman among her people.

Mattie leaned close and peered into his eyes. "Hold still," she said when he tried to shy away.

"Mattie, what's up?"

"That," she said in a tone of great portent, "is what I'm trying to find out."

"I think it's time for you to rest like the doctor ordered," he told her.

"On the other hand, it might be time for you and me to have a little talk." Mattie's eyes glinted with humor. "If you're going to fall in love, I'd like to give you some pointers."

"Too little too late," he said with what he hoped was a note of finality. He wasn't ready to tell her that he had a permanent case of heartbreak, and he didn't think he'd ever recover.

"What do you mean, too little too late?" Mattie asked sharply.

"I met a wonderful woman, Mattie. And then I lost her. My fault entirely." In his mind, he pictured Brooke, her blond hair blowing in the breeze through the open windows of the Jeep, her eyes so deep and blue at the height of lovemaking, the slight rounding of her abdomen where the baby was.

"Can you fix what happened?"

"She's gone, Mattie. I can't find her." He'd bombarded her apartment in L.A. with phone calls; he'd failed to find her e-mail address on the Internet; he'd even left a message at *Fling* magazine for her to call him, for whatever good it would do.

Mattie's face clouded. "That's too bad. It would please me to see you settled before—"

"Before what?" he demanded. "You're not thinking of moving back to the reservation, are you?"

"When you're going to live here with us? No, I like it here, and Glenna will make my life easier. It's not that, Cord."

"What is it, then?"

She assessed him with a long, penetrating look. "I was hoping you'd adopt Jonathan, Cord. He loves you so."

"Adopt Jonny?" The idea had never occurred to him, and his reaction was immediately negative. He'd never thought he'd be a good father, since his father had set such a bad example.

"Adopting Jonathan would be good for both of you. Ever since my son and daughter-in-law died, he's missed being part of a family."

"He lucked out when he came to live with you, Mattie."

"I love Jonathan dearly. I worry about the future, that's all. My health isn't so good anymore, Cord. I don't know how long I'll last." Her bottom lip quivered, but she didn't break down. She was a strong woman, was Mattie.

"You'll be around for a good long time, I'm sure. Don't talk like that. You're my best girl, you know."

"I'm your only girl for now, but you'll find someone else someday. Maybe not the one you lost, but somebody. I'd like to see you settled with a family, you and your wife and Jonathan."

He tentatively tried the idea on for size. A family. Husband, wife and child. If he married Brooke, they would add her baby to the mix. After all his years of foster homes, of wandering, a family was almost too much to hope for. It was something that happened to other lucky people, not to him, and the thought of what he had been missing all these long years tugged at his heart.

"You'll think about adopting Jonathan, Cord?"

He couldn't bear to disappoint Mattie, of all people. He patted her hand. "Sure, Mattie. I'll think about it," he said.

# Chapter Twelve

Brooke's one-bedroom apartment seemed lonely and empty after she returned from Rancho Encantado. She unpacked her work materials, glancing at the leather pouch that held the old scrolls. She didn't speak Spanish, but perhaps she could have them translated soon. She tossed the pouch to the back of her closet and tried to settle down to work, even unplugging the phone thinking that an absence of interruptions would help her concentrate.

Nothing worked. She missed Cord, and she wanted more than anything to be with him. She wondered if she had said or done anything to make him pull away from her when they had become as close as a man and woman could be. Making love had boosted them into a whole different dimension, or had it? It wasn't the first time she'd misjudged the situation, that was for sure.

As she was unpacking, she unwrapped the china doll that she'd found in the cave. She set it carefully on her dresser. The glass eyes stared unblinkingly, reminding her that she needed to finish reading Jerusha

Taggart's diary. By this time, she felt as if she and Jerusha were old friends, so she settled down in her favorite chair to read in the hope that it would help her to stop obsessing about Cord McCall.

January 23, 1850

Today my beloved friend Annabel Privette breathed her last.

All of our party has survived the winter in these caves so far, though we suffer greatly from the cold. Annabel has been ill since before leaving her home in Ohio, but she bravely set out on this journey because her husband wished it and because of the promise of a better life for her three children. I will not set down the gruesome details of her illness, except to say that it was surely consumption and that it was so far advanced that she would certainly not have lived even if she had not undertaken this journey.

Our wagon master, Mr. Tyson, is much saddened by Annabel's death. He has worked mightily to keep us fed, finding game where we thought there was none, making sure that Annabel and all the children got the best of the food.

We have learned that the Hennessy contingent, which broke with our party when we entered the great desert, has suffered more than we have. Mr. Tyson encountered some of their number when he was hunting one day and says they are camped in caves similar to ours some miles away. Many of those poor misguided souls have died of starvation. Mr. Tyson took a side of venison to them yesterday and left it where they would find it. He believes that his adversary, Mr. Hennessy, is ill, as are many of the children. There is no talk of their rejoining us. Perhaps if Mr. Hennessy dies, we will all band together for our common good.

I will miss my dear friend Annabel Privette. Now I must sadly turn my attention to her children, who grieve the loss of their mother.

Brooke scribbled a few notes, mostly about Tyson. All the accounts that she had read about the Cedrella Pass situation had portrayed Tyson as the person responsible for a great deal of suffering. Yet here was an assertion by Jerusha, herself a member of his party, that Tyson looked after the Hennessy group as well as his own. It was a new point of view, one that could be important to her book.

A glance at the clock told her that it was time to switch to the Rancho Encantado piece. She dreaded working on it, since there was only that lead staring her in the face.

Certainly, she had nothing bad to say about the place. She'd detected no false hype, had found the lost legend a charming bit of trivia, and as for the vortex, people would believe what they liked. Maybe there was a ghost, but if so, he was benign. Even after the understandable confusion on the day she'd arrived, her experience at the ranch had been totally pleasant.

She stared at her lead.

*There is nothing special about Rancho Encantado.*
The piece should have ended there, but to Brooke's

amazement, there were more words unfolding beneath the lead. She went on reading.

There is nothing special about Rancho Encantado. Unless you consider the fabled makeovers, which have given so many women the look they've always wanted. Unless you count the relaxing massages, the yoga classes, and did I mention the oasis hot pool?

People come from all over the country to experience the amenities of this health spa and dude ranch in the Seven Springs area of the California desert. Desert, you say? What's so special about the desert?

Well, Rancho Encantado is set in a jewel-like valley smack in the middle of one of the driest places on earth. Mountains to the east, mountains to the west, and—

Brooke blinked at her computer screen in disbelief. She hadn't written those words. She scrolled through the article. Why, it was well written, and in her own unique style. How could this have happened?

She reached the end of the piece and sat back in her chair in bewilderment. Except for the odd turn of phrase, the article was ready to present to Felice.

She punched a couple of buttons, and when the piece was printed, she began to proofread it, but her attention was diverted when her computer signaled that a new document was opening. Again, it was one that she'd never seen before in her life.

## Padre Luís Writes

Brooke, my child! I believe that you can read this. I am but a poor humble priest, and little do I know of writing. However, I somehow found myself with the ability to complete the article about Rancho Encantado so that you can return to us. I do not know how, but the words came to me, and now they have appeared in this little book where you write. Many times I have tried to reach you in this manner, but never have I succeeded until now. God works in miraculous ways, especially in this blessed place.

Now that your article for that magazine is written, you will surely be free to return to Rancho Encantado. You need to continue your research so you can write your book about the women of Cedrella Pass. And Cord needs you. He needs you more than you can know. He needs you even more than you need him.

I cannot explain further. I am, after all, only an intermediary in this matter. Please, please, come back

here. For your sake and Cord's and for that of your
unborn child. Soon, Brooke. Soon.
Your humble servant,
Luís Reyes de Santiago

Brooke shook her head to clear it, sure that she must
be dreaming. But the words didn't disappear from her
screen. She didn't wake up. The letter from Padre Luís
was real.

Brooke didn't stop to question what he had written.
She didn't think of doubting that there was a ghostly
priest and that he had found a way to contact her at
home in L.A. In fact, she wasted no time in packing
up her computer and throwing clean clothes into her
small suitcase. In less than half an hour she was on
the freeway, leaving L.A., headed back to Rancho Encantado and Cord.

THIS TIME she was offered one of the guest suites in
Sagebrush, but Brooke asked for the apartment in the
stable, instead.

"I suppose you'll be wanting to see Cord again,"
Bridget said as she handed her the key.

"I'll be researching things on my own from now
on," Brooke said, avoiding a straight answer.

"I see," Bridget said speculatively. She added, "In
that case, I suppose it won't matter to you that Cord
has left."

"Left?" This information caught her by surprise.

"He's not employed at Rancho Encantado anymore."

"Did—did he say where he was going?"

"If he did, I haven't heard." At that point, several

new guests arrived, commanding Bridget's attention, and Brooke seized the opportunity to escape.

As she wheeled her suitcase toward the stable, she contemplated what Cord had told her about his plans. Only that he would be going away soon, and he'd avoided saying anything more. Now she might never know what had happened to him. But she was determined not to dwell on that; it was time to move on with her life.

In the apartment that she would occupy again, she thankfully found everything the same as it had been. The comfortable couch with the afghan, the television in the pie safe, the alcove where she worked—all seemed warm and welcoming. After she set up her computer and unpacked her clothes, she settled on the couch to read the rest of Jerusha Taggart's diary.

March 13, 1850

I write this as I sit in a warm kitchen surrounded by my children and the Privette family, as well. We are safe at last. Rescuers managed to reach us last week, and we were brought out of Cedrella Pass. We could not help thinking about the curse of the Mojave woman. Did it play a part in our being trapped in the caves for so long with so little to eat? I do not know, nor does anyone else.

All of the Tyson group except poor Annabel survived the ordeal. James Privette has a cold, but it is not serious and we expect him to recover.

As for me, I delight in the children's laughter, and I joyfully await the birth of my child. If it is a girl, I will name her Annabel; if a boy, Charles, which is a name that I admire greatly.

We will never forget our ordeal at Cedrella Pass, but we face the future stronger for it. If we can survive such hardship, there is nothing that can stop us now.

Brooke paused in her reading, then turned the page.

April 25, 1850
Today I gave birth to my third child, Charles. He is a fine strong boy.

There were no more entries until July of that year.

July 30, 1850
Finally, we have reached the goldfields! Teensy, who now demands to be called by her given name, Olivia, is the most excited. She has met a friend here, a lovely girl about her age, and perhaps the friendship will stop her mourning the loss of her beloved Eliza, the doll that somehow was left behind at Cedrella Pass during the confusion of our rescue. Nathan is still much weakened by our privations, but I feel that the good food that we are able to obtain here will nourish him into better health. The baby, Charles, continues to gain weight.

My dear husband comes to inform me that our neighbors have delivered a large ham as a welcoming gift. Now I must go thank them and serve it to my family. It was not so long ago that we almost starved, so I am most grateful for this provenance.

Truly, our long ordeal is over.

Brooke closed the cover of the diary. Now she knew that the Taggarts had made it to the goldfields, and she knew that James Privette and his family had arrived there later. The Privettes, although they had prospered in their new home, had not struck it rich. Perhaps the Taggarts had; she hoped so.

She got up and stretched. No sounds came from the apartment next door, which only reminded her that its occupant was gone and forever lost to her.

"But I have you," she said to her baby. She now carried on a real dialogue with this baby, and the fact that she had reached this present comfort level with her pregnancy was due to Cord. He had generously and gently pushed her toward the realization that her pregnancy was not just a burden; it was a gift. She wished she could thank him for that, but she would probably never get the chance.

*You will,* said the voice that she had heard so many times now. She whirled, expecting to see the figure of the priest standing behind her, but of course no one was there.

BROOKE SLEPT late the next morning. In midmorning she got up, ate a few saltines and decided to risk breakfast. Afterward, she took a quick shower and started entering her notes on the Jeffords interview into her computer.

It was later, when she was taking a work break, that she saw the boy through the bathroom window. He was a skinny kid with a backpack, maybe twelve or thirteen years old, and he was trudging along the path from the barn as if too tired to go on. He seemed out of place here, too young to be working with the cattle, and she didn't recognize him as one of the employees' kids whom she'd noticed playing on the grounds during her previous stay.

She watched him for a few minutes, then went to the bedroom to dress. As she pulled a T-shirt over her head, she heard a noise outside the kitchen door, a kind of thump, which made her curious enough to open it. There was the boy, dejectedly sitting on her top step. He jumped to his feet when she opened the door.

"Sorry, ma'am, I thought this apartment was empty like the one next door." There was something appealing about him, she thought. He had an open face, a sweet vulnerability, never mind that she detected a false bravado.

"Can I help you find someone?" she asked. Maybe he was here to inquire about an after-school job. Come to think of it, why wasn't he in school right now?

"I'm looking for Bucky," he said.

"Bucky? Oh, you must mean Cord."

"That's it. He's not home." The boy looked so discouraged that she felt as though she should offer help.

"Cord doesn't work here anymore."

"Oh." The boy's face fell.

"I'm sorry, but I don't know where he went."

He picked up his backpack, which was much too big for him. "Someone told me where he might be. It's far, but I know the way." He turned to go.

*He's hungry,* said the voice that she now believed

belonged to the ghost of Padre Luís. This time she didn't wonder about it, and she didn't miss a beat.

"Um, I don't suppose you'd like something to eat," she said.

"Wow, I sure would. I mean, if it wouldn't be too much trouble."

"I don't have much food, only what I picked up along the way from L.A. yesterday. I can offer you a bowl of cereal, that's for sure. By the way, my name's Brooke Hollister."

"Mine's Brandon. Nice to meet you," he said. Hesitantly, he followed her inside and slung his backpack on a kitchen chair. Brooke poured orange juice and cereal and he wolfed down one bowlful, then two. He drained the juice in a few gulps.

"I could make you some toast." She was sorry she didn't have more to offer, but she'd only stocked the essentials.

"Oh, thanks, that would be great."

Curious about what had brought him here and wondering why he thought he knew where Cord was, she fixed him two pieces of cinnamon toast and sat down across the table from him.

"You're planning to walk to where you can find Cord?" she asked carefully.

He grinned at her, a flash of white teeth in a freckled face. "Sure, I can do it. Maybe I'll get lucky and hitch a ride."

"I don't think that's a good idea," she said. "It's not safe."

"Hitchhiking's the best way for a kid like me to get around," he said defensively.

Brooke knew instinctively not to ask about Brandon's parents. She suspected that he was a runaway, and she had written articles about runaways. She understood all too well how such kids often found themselves in a lot of trouble.

"How do you know Cord?" she asked, hoping she wasn't acting like the kind of prying adult Brandon might be trying to avoid.

"I don't exactly. Judge—well, I've heard about him. I decided I needed to see him real bad." The boy shifted uncomfortably in his chair, looking as if he thought he'd revealed too much. "I'd better be going," he added.

Brooke was on her feet before he was. "Wait, Brandon. I'll be glad to take you to Cord. You said you know the way, right?"

"Sure, Judge Petty told me about Bucky's ranch. I don't want to cause you any trouble, though."

"It's no trouble," Brooke said firmly. She went and got her jacket from the closet. "Come on, let's go." Cord hadn't mentioned a ranch to her, but it made sense. What didn't make sense was why he hadn't confided in her.

Brandon seemed delighted at this stroke of luck. "This is great, Brooke. You don't mind if I call you that?" He kept up a stream of chatter until he saw her sporty car, which made his eyes open wide in appreciation, and then he talked even more.

Brooke was happy to keep him talking. It kept her from thinking about seeing Cord again and wondering what he would say when he saw her.

CORD, who was stacking scraps of lumber behind the Jornada Ranch barn, glanced up when he saw the red sports car pulling a plume of dust toward him on the road from the highway. At first, he didn't believe his eyes. Then he decided that it was someone else's car, not Brooke's. But when she drove through the open gate and he saw her bright hair gleaming in the mid-afternoon sun, he knew who it was, all right. His mind couldn't compute the scruffy kid who climbed out of the passenger side of the car, and he didn't want to look at him anyway. He could only stare at Brooke and wonder how on earth she had tracked him down.

He wiped his hands on a rag and strode forward. She stood quietly by the car, her hair ruffled into a pale-gold tangle by the breeze blowing in from the mountains, and he couldn't wait to bury his face in it, to run his fingers through it, to smell its fresh sun-washed scent. She was taking in the sprawling ranch house, the new roof on the bunkhouse, and wore jeans that hugged her derriere and showed the slight rounding of her belly.

Probably no one else would detect that she was pregnant, but he saw because he knew. And in that moment he knew one other thing that made his heart leap with gladness. He knew he wanted her baby, wanted to make it his own. Wanted to make Brooke his own, and Jonathan, too.

He came to a stop in front of her. Her eyes searched his face, seeking—reassurance? Love? Oh, there was a plenitude of that in his heart. There was enough to go around, enough for all of them.

He heard, as if from a long way away, the boy's voice. "Bucky?"

Recognizing his long-ago nickname, he pulled his eyes away from Brooke with great effort and focused them on her companion. The kid sported a chopped-off haircut that looked like his own handiwork and wore clothes that were too small. The boy's eyes were what got him, though. They were eyes old before their time, eyes like the ones he'd seen every time he'd looked in the mirror when he was that age.

"My name's Brandon Wittich. Judge Petty called you about me."

Cord remembered that phone call and how he'd told Ted Petty that the ranch wasn't ready to receive boys. Brandon was the kid Ted had mentioned, the one from the bad home who needed a place to stay.

"I remember," he said.

"I need to talk to you." The boy's expression was one of desperation, of making a last-ditch attempt.

He wanted nothing more than to go to Brooke and gather her into his arms, but he said to the kid, "Let's go inside and have a talk."

Brooke made a move as if to climb back into her car. He reached out and rested his hand on her arm. "You, too," he said.

He thought for a moment that she was going to object, but when their eyes met, he saw that tears quivered on the tips of her eyelashes. She didn't say anything, only nodded. He slid one arm around her and rested the other hand on Brandon's slight shoulder, and they walked like that, together, into the house.

BROOKE MET MATTIE as soon as the three of them entered the spacious living room. Mattie, who hurried in from the kitchen, was shadowed by an appealing dark-eyed moppet of a boy, who grinned engagingly as Cord made quick introductions.

"Brandon and I are going into the living room," Cord said. "We'll need some privacy, but don't go too far away." His eyes caught and held Brooke's.

Mattie immediately rose to the occasion. "Come with me," she said, curving an arm around Brooke's waist. "Jonathan and I made cookies this morning, and the three of us will sit down and visit for a while."

"Maybe she could play Mr. Mouth with me," Jonathan said hopefully. Brooke smiled at him, charmed by what she saw. He was only about five, but his eyes sparkled with a lively intelligence, and he seemed to warm to her right away. He reached for her hand as if he'd known her all his life.

"Later, Jonathan. Right now we want to get acquainted," Mattie told him, but he kept hold of Brooke's hand anyway.

The kitchen was equipped with new appliances and a shiny wood floor, where Jonathan immediately busied himself playing toy cars.

Brooke filled Mattie in about the *Fling* article that had brought her to Rancho Encantado and told her about the book she planned to write about the women of Cedrella Pass. Mattie had nothing but enthusiasm about the book and wasted no time in mentioning that she was half Shoshone.

"My mother is the one who removed the curse from the valley," she said with an air of pride.

Brooke's eyes widened. "You know something about the lost legend?"

Mattie grinned. "The legend isn't lost. It's the scroll that's lost."

"That's not what I heard. Justine didn't know what the legend was about."

"Justine is relatively new to the valley. The legend was supposedly written on an old scroll that Padre Luís gave to the Iversons, the homesteaders who couldn't make a go of ranching. He delivered it at the same time that he delivered an old deed, and no one has seen either one since."

Brooke recalled the scrolls in the leather pouch that she'd found in the old humpbacked trunk. To know that perhaps she was the one who had found the deed and the lost legend was exciting.

"How did you learn so much about the history of Rancho Encantado?" she asked Mattie.

"The Shoshone tribe was here long before anyone else, dear. My mother heard the legend from her relatives, all tribal members. They kept the legend alive by word of mouth."

"Tell me more about the legend," she said.

Mattie pushed the plate of cookies across the table to her, and Brooke took one.

"You know about the ill-fated Forty-niners who tried to cross the mountains at Cedrella Pass in the dead of winter?"

Brooke, her mouth full of cookie, nodded.

"Well, the legend has it that the Tyson party captured a couple of Mojave braves and held them hostage until they told them where in the desert they could find water. When the braves led them to their village and the spring nearby, the only person in residence was an old Mojave woman. She was so angry about the men's being held hostage that she cursed the Tyson party and everyone in it. The more superstitious of the travelers blamed the curse for the hardships that followed. And they blamed Tyson, of course.''

Brooke was excited to hear almost the same version of this episode as Jerusha had reported in her diary. ''I've uncovered a first-person account that makes me think that the newspaper stories of the time were wrong to place all the blame on Willis Tyson. I think the reporters interviewed survivors of the Hennessy group, who blamed Tyson for their predicament, and no one ever contradicted them. Tyson was a scapegoat.''

Mattie looked interested. ''If that's the case, Cord will be happy to hear it.''

It was on the tip of Brooke's tongue to ask why, but Mattie went on talking.

''Anyway, back to the legend. Padre Luís, who was a great friend to the Shoshone, never thought that the curse delivered by the old woman at the Mojave camp amounted to anything. He said that good works and love could overcome any obstacle. My mother was not so sure. She said a wisewoman of the Mojaves had delivered the curse and only another wisewoman could remove it, so she called on the Great Spirit to bless the valley and all who entered. My mother had shamanistic powers, you see. She always said that there was strong medicine in the valley.''

''Did she say it was a vortex?''

"A vortex? My mother wouldn't have known the word, but I don't think it matters what you call it. There are places on this earth where unusual and unexpected things happen."

"I wouldn't have believed that was true until they happened to me."

Mattie nailed Brooke with a meaningful look. "You came to Rancho Encantado needing love."

"How do you know that?" Brooke stared. She had, after all, just met this woman.

Mattie smiled indulgently. "I have my ways. You are going to have a baby, and you needed to love the child in order to bear it and raise it. You didn't realize that at first, did you?"

Brooke shook her head. "I do now," she said quietly.

"When you arrived in the valley, you thought that the only love worth having was that between a man and a woman, I think."

"Yes," Brooke whispered. "The baby's father didn't want me."

"Ah, Brooke, now you see that he doesn't matter. You have your child and the love that child brings into your life."

"What about Cord? What about the love I feel for him?"

"All love is bound together, Brooke, don't you see? It is of one piece—God's love and our love for one another."

"You are a very wise woman yourself, Mattie."

"Rancho Encantado is where dreams come true.

Your dreams will come true, and that's all I will say about that.''

"I wish I could be sure."

Mattie patted her hand. "Cord loves you. All you have to do now is let it happen."

Let what happen? Whatever it was, Brooke hoped it would be soon.

LATER, WHILE JONATHAN was showing her his room, Brooke overheard Cord talking on the telephone.

"Ted, we can't allow Brandon to go back home. He can stay here in Jonathan's room overnight but Jornada Ranch could be open for business as soon as we get state agency approval."

He listened for a minute or so. "Anything you can do to speed up licensure will be appreciated. Yeah, Brandon is a great kid. I think he'd do well here."

Brooke was distracted by Jonathan's rock collection, so she missed the end of the conversation, but soon Cord poked his head in the door.

"Jonathan, you're going to have a guest. Let's get your top bunk made up for Brandon," Cord said.

Jonathan let out an excited whoop. "I'll go get the sheets from Granny," he said. He ran out, calling for Mattie.

Brooke stood awkwardly in the middle of the room, unable to look away from Cord, her exit blocked by him.

Cord looked sheepish and ran a hand through his hair. "Now you're onto my secret," he said. "Jornada Ranch."

"Cord, it's beautiful here. The mountains in the distance, the cottonwoods along the creek—I don't understand why you kept it from me.''

"I'm not used to confiding in anyone. The old issue of trust, I guess. When I was growing up I learned not to talk to people because anything I said could be used against me and often was." He shrugged. "Brooke, this place is important to me. I'm going to take in boys who have difficult home lives. They'll live here, have three square meals a day, and learn to work with horses.''

"I admire you," Brooke said. "I can't tell you how much.''

He took her hand and pulled her down beside him on the lower bunk. "There's a reason I'm doing this. I landed on a ranch during the worst time of my life. I lived there with a family named McCall. Working with horses became a kind of therapy. I liked taking care of them, and I liked riding them. I want to give other kids the same kind of chance.''

"You were adopted by these people? Your name's the same.''

Cord shook his head. "They pulled up stakes and moved to Montana when I was fifteen. I couldn't go with them because I wasn't old enough to be released from the state foster-care system. I was sent to another family, who were really awful. They were in it for the money, and kids like me were their meal ticket. Anyway, when I struck out on my own, I took the name McCall and wouldn't answer to Bucky anymore. My middle name was Cord, and as for my former last name, well, I was glad to get rid of that, too. I was born a Tyson, Brooke.''

She stared at him. "Any relation to Willis Tyson, the wagon master?"

"I'm a direct descendant. Around here, Tysons were considered no damn good. Me included. My father was a drunk, and my uncle was in jail for burglary. My grandfather shot a man in cold blood. He was a descendant of Willis Tyson, the guy everyone around here blamed for the Cedrella Pass deaths. I never knew a Tyson who was decent and good." His tone was bitter.

"You are," Brooke said softly.

"I haven't always behaved myself," he reminded her.

"Cord, what if I told you that Willis Tyson wasn't as bad as they say?"

He turned her hand over and traced the lines. "I'd listen. I'm not sure I'd believe."

"Jerusha wrote admiringly of him in her diary. She says he tried to help the Hennessy group." She told him a few more details, and his eyes began to take on an expression of amazement.

"If that's true, it's great news."

"I'm going to corroborate it. There may be other records where no one's thought to look. All the published accounts of the incident seem to derive from one or two articles written after the people were rescued from the pass. If the reporter only talked to members of the Hennessy group, those were hardly unbiased accounts."

Jonathan returned bearing an armload of clean, folded sheets. "Here you are, Cord," he said.

"Jonny, go ask Brandon if he wants to watch TV with you while Brooke and I make up the bed."

Jonathan raced away, and they heard the TV switch on. Brooke unfolded the sheets, and they spread them out on the top bunk.

"I've missed you, Brooke," Cord said.

She was glad that she was occupied with making the bed. It made it easier to keep her emotions in check. "I had to leave. The Jeffords interview—"

"I know," Cord said. "Justine told me. I tried to call you in L.A., but you didn't answer the phone."

"Sometimes I don't when I'm working. I wasn't expecting a call from you." She concentrated on making a hospital tuck on the bottom corner of the sheet.

"You didn't think I'd call? After what happened that night in the cave?"

"After you said you needed more space," she corrected firmly.

Cord stopped spreading the blanket and stared at her. "I said I needed time out because I freaked after seeing the place where all those people died because of Willis Tyson."

"But—"

"Before today, I've never heard anything positive about Tyson. About *any* Tyson, Brooke. Being there brought forth all the old anger and guilt that I felt when I was a Tyson."

"I didn't know," Brooke said, stricken. She would

never have insisted that he take her to Cedrella Pass if she'd realized why he didn't want to go.

"I should have told you. I should have told you a lot of things. For instance, that I love you." He gazed at her, and her heart started skipping beats. His hands came up to her shoulders, and turned her gently toward him. "I love you, Brooke," he repeated, and then he kissed her.

It was a sweet and tender kiss, and she leaned into it as his arms went around her to hold her close. In the background they heard music from the TV, the clatter of dishes as Mattie set the kitchen table for supper, Jonathan's chortle over something Brandon said. At the moment, these seemed like the most romantic sounds in the world.

They broke apart self-consciously, knowing that someone could walk in at any minute.

"I love you, too," Brooke said helplessly. "Now what?"

Cord grinned at her and kissed the tip of her nose. "We'll talk about that after supper," he said.

THE LITTLE STREAM behind the bunkhouse purled gently at their feet, and the moon shone full above. Cord, when Mattie wasn't looking, had filched a couple of blankets from the linen closet, and he spread them on a soft bed of leaves.

Brooke sat down and held her arms out to him. He came to her then and wrapped her tightly in his arms.

"You know why I named this place Jornada Ranch?" he asked.

She shook her head. With all that had happened today, it was the last thing she'd wondered.

"*Jornada* means 'journey' in Spanish. The boys who come here will be on a journey to find themselves, and I'll be their guide. I want you to be my companion along the way, Brooke. I don't want to lose you again. Will you marry me?"

She leaned back to find that he was staring at her so compellingly that she couldn't look away. For a moment she allowed herself to think about what marriage to Cord would entail: moving out of L.A., leaving her friends, growing accustomed to living on a ranch that was home to the boys that Cord intended to help. And she knew that this was a better life than the one she had, was better by far than life with Leo would have been. It would be a good life for her baby, as well.

And she loved this man. She knew that for sure.

"Yes," she murmured. "I'll marry you, Cord."

He smiled down at her. "All right. It's settled." His face clouded for a moment. "There's only one thing more. Jonathan. Mattie asked me to adopt him."

"And you said what?"

"I said I'd think about it."

The words that Mattie had spoken ran through Brooke's head. *All love is bound together…it is of one piece…God's love and our love for one another.* If she loved Cord, then she surely loved the other people he loved. Jonathan, Mattie, the boys whose lives would be changed by what he planned to do here.

In that moment, she felt her heart expand as if to contain the whole universe. "Let's go for it," she said.

"It'll be a big family," he warned.

"A happy family," she said.

"Dear Brooke, I love you so much."

"Prove it," she said, pulling him down on the blankets beside her.

The night was cool, but they had each other for warmth. This time there was no hesitation, only the sweet knowledge that this was right for both of them. One blanket over them, one blanket under them, they undressed and settled into each other's arms.

"Oh, Cord," Brooke whispered. "This is so good."

"You bet," he said.

Slowly, he began to explore her body, kissing her breasts, her lips, her eyelids and feathering a string of kisses across her throat. Brooke closed her eyes, letting herself be absorbed in him, drinking him into every pore, feeling the rightness of this new relationship that they had forged.

He tangled his fingers in her hair, his breath caressing her cheek. He sighed in contentment as he found her center, slid in, began to rock in a rhythm that soothed her soul. She spun into it, merged with him, let herself be borne away on a warm gentle wind toward the moon and stars, and the stars wheeled higher and higher into the heavens, bursting inside her, a thousand stars sparking all her nerve endings and making her so hot that she had to let go, had to fall away with Cord, falling until she could breathe again, until all she knew of the world was that Cord loved her as much as she loved him.

Afterward, she traced lazy circles on his back, her fingers pausing to explore the scars where steel rods had been inserted in his vertebrae. "Do these scars hurt?" she asked.

"No, not to touch. I have aches and pains sometimes, but I don't mind. It's preferable to never walking again. I was lucky."

"If you hadn't had the accident, you'd still be with the rodeo. We'd never have met."

"If I hadn't had the accident, Jornada Ranch wouldn't exist. I was able to buy the property with the big insurance settlement I got."

"Good things come from bad experiences sometimes," she said, thinking of Leo's rejection.

"Like this ranch. Like your baby. Our baby now," he said, patting her stomach.

"You know, I've been thinking about the Rancho Encantado motto," she said.

"Why?" he asked, clearly surprised.

She shifted away from him, her arms around his neck. His eyes danced in the moonlight, and she smiled. "Rancho Encantado, Where Dreams Come True. It happened for me, Cord."

"And me," he said in some surprise.

"It's a magical place."

"I'm a believer now that I've found a woman I love with all my heart," he said.

"And where might she be?"

"Right here in my arms," he said.

"Which is exactly where she intends to stay for the rest of her life," Brooke said, and she raised her lips for his kiss.

For a moment, out of the corner of her eye, she thought she saw the benign figure of the little priest in the branches of the cottonwood tree, and he was giving her a thumbs-up sign. But when she looked again, he was gone.

## Padre Luís Thinks

*One year later*

Now that Brooke and Cord have been married for almost a year, I can stop worrying about them. They have their baby daughter, Felicity, who is named for Brooke's friend Felice. They have their son, Jonathan, who visits his grandmother, Mattie, almost every day on his way home from school.

And they have ready baby-sitters in the boys, all twelve of them.

Brandon was the first, and he is doing well. Now there are lots of boys and lots of fun. When I hear their laughter it makes me wish I were a child again. And the horses! They benefit greatly from the attention. Cord has taken in abused horses that need the love that these boys can give. Oh, it is quite something, this Jornada Ranch.

Brooke has settled happily into her new life. Mattie's niece Glenna looks after the house so that Brooke can work on her book about the women of Cedrella Pass. This is good. I have long believed that the pioneer women have not been given enough credit for the westward expansion of the nation. They were strong and steadfast, ready to go the last mile for the men and children they loved. Like Brooke, in other words.

Though she did not know it at first, Brooke came to Rancho Encantado to learn that love is the answer. But she would not have had to come to this place to discover love. It was inside her all the time, buried deep in her heart. It's so simple, really. Why do people not see? Why must this simple truth be pointed out to them over and over again?

*Por Dios,* if everyone got the message, I suppose that there would be nothing left for me to do. Clearly I will have my work cut out for me in this place forever.

But if that is God's will, then who am I to object? I am happy to be the messenger, and I am more than happy to be a poor humble priest serving in any way I can.

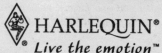

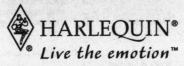

**Your opinion is important to us!** Please take a few moments to share your thoughts with us about your experiences with Harlequin and Silhouette books. Your comments will be very useful in ensuring that we deliver books you love to read.
*Please take a few minutes to complete the questionnaire, then send it to us at the address below.*

Send your completed questionnaires to:
**Harlequin/Silhouette Reader Survey, P.O. Box 9046, Buffalo, NY 14269-9046**

1. As you may know, there are many different lines under the Harlequin and Silhouette brands. Each of the lines is listed below. Please check the box that most represents your reading habit for each line.

| Line | Currently read this line | Do not read this line | Not sure if I read this line |
|---|---|---|---|
| Harlequin American Romance | ❏ | ❏ | ❏ |
| Harlequin Duets | ❏ | ❏ | ❏ |
| Harlequin Romance | ❏ | ❏ | ❏ |
| Harlequin Historicals | ❏ | ❏ | ❏ |
| Harlequin Superromance | ❏ | ❏ | ❏ |
| Harlequin Intrigue | ❏ | ❏ | ❏ |
| Harlequin Presents | ❏ | ❏ | ❏ |
| Harlequin Temptation | ❏ | ❏ | ❏ |
| Harlequin Blaze | ❏ | ❏ | ❏ |
| Silhouette Special Edition | ❏ | ❏ | ❏ |
| Silhouette Romance | ❏ | ❏ | ❏ |
| Silhouette Intimate Moments | ❏ | ❏ | ❏ |
| Silhouette Desire | ❏ | ❏ | ❏ |

2. Which of the following best describes why you bought *this book?* One answer only, please.

| | | | |
|---|---|---|---|
| the picture on the cover | ❏ | the title | ❏ |
| the author | ❏ | the line is one I read often | ❏ |
| part of a miniseries | ❏ | saw an ad in another book | ❏ |
| saw an ad in a magazine/newsletter | ❏ | a friend told me about it | ❏ |
| I borrowed/was given this book | ❏ | other: _____ | ❏ |

3. Where did you buy *this book?* One answer only, please.

| | | | |
|---|---|---|---|
| at Barnes & Noble | ❏ | at a grocery store | ❏ |
| at Waldenbooks | ❏ | at a drugstore | ❏ |
| at Borders | ❏ | on eHarlequin.com Web site | ❏ |
| at another bookstore | ❏ | from another Web site | ❏ |
| at Wal-Mart | ❏ | Harlequin/Silhouette Reader | ❏ |
| at Target | ❏ | Service/through the mail | |
| at Kmart | ❏ | used books from anywhere | ❏ |
| at another department store or mass merchandiser | ❏ | I borrowed/was given this book | ❏ |

4. On average, how many Harlequin and Silhouette books do you buy at one time?

| | |
|---|---|
| I buy _____ books at one time | ❏ |
| I rarely buy a book | ❏ |

MRQ403HAR-1A

5. How many times per month do you shop for any *Harlequin and/or Silhouette* books?
One answer only, please.

| | | | |
|---|---|---|---|
| 1 or more times a week | ❑ | a few times per year | ❑ |
| 1 to 3 times per month | ❑ | less often than once a year | ❑ |
| 1 to 2 times every 3 months | ❑ | never | ❑ |

6. When you think of your ideal heroine, which *one* statement describes her the best?
One answer only, please.

| | | | |
|---|---|---|---|
| She's a woman who is strong-willed | ❑ | She's a desirable woman | ❑ |
| She's a woman who is needed by others | ❑ | She's a powerful woman | ❑ |
| She's a woman who is taken care of | ❑ | She's a passionate woman | ❑ |
| She's an adventurous woman | | She's a sensitive woman | ❑ |

7. The following statements describe types or genres of books that you may be interested in reading. Pick *up to 2 types* of books that you are most interested in.

| | |
|---|---|
| I like to read about truly romantic relationships | ❑ |
| I like to read stories that are sexy romances | ❑ |
| I like to read romantic comedies | ❑ |
| I like to read a romantic mystery/suspense | ❑ |
| I like to read about romantic adventures | ❑ |
| I like to read romance stories that involve family | ❑ |
| I like to read about a romance in times or places that I have never seen | ❑ |
| Other: _____ | ❑ |

*The following questions help us to group your answers with those readers who are similar to you. Your answers will remain confidential.*

8. Please record your year of birth below.
19 ____

9. What is your marital status?

single ❑     married ❑     common-law ❑     widowed ❑
divorced/separated ❑

10. Do you have children 18 years of age or younger currently living at home?
yes ❑     no ❑

11. Which of the following best describes your employment status?

employed full-time or part-time ❑     homemaker ❑     student ❑
retired ❑     unemployed ❑

12. Do you have access to the Internet from either home or work?
yes ❑     no ❑

13. Have you ever visited eHarlequin.com?
yes ❑     no ❑

14. What state do you live in?
_____

15. Are you a member of Harlequin/Silhouette Reader Service?

yes ❑     Account # _____     no ❑     MRQ403HAR-1B

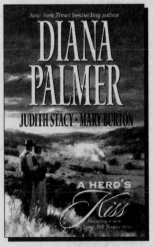

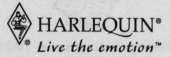